Fields of Alicia

Lee DuCote

ISBN: 978-1-4834-1925-1 (sc)
ISBN: 978-1-4834-1924-4 (e)

Managing Editor: Alice Sullivan alicesullivan.com

Lulu Publishing Services rev. date: 10/10/2014

To my best friend and wife, Alicia, who was named after her father's favorite hay fields.

Thank you to my family, Alicia, Dylan, Shannon, and Tucker, for allowing my absence while writing and constantly cheering for my dreams. Let the adventure begin!

My profound thanks to my coach and editor whom I have the great luxury of working with: Alice Sullivan.

To a great team at Lulu publishing for being so easy to work with and caring that this story is shared.

Chapter 1

Lying in a hay field, Madi watched as the clouds hovered; the warm breeze folded the blue-tinted grass over her body as it passed through the field. She had spent many hours like this in her father's award-winning hay field. Too many to remember—or forget.

Established in the early 1920s, Hamlin Farms was notorious for its Alicia Bermuda hay. Three times a year farmers and ranchers would come from all over the South to buy the high-yielding hay. There weren't too many farmers who knew how to grow the hay successfully, and the Hamlin family had figured it out.

Madi patiently waited for the next cloud to form so she could add it to her collection of imaginational animals. Closing her eyes she could feel the tears welling up, ready at any moment to weave warm streams of memories down her face. But the next gust of wind blew her long blonde hair in her eyes and put her at peace. Growing up on a hay farm she liked to believe that the blue-tinted field had magical powers that could take her anywhere in the world. Many times she would close her eyes and envision the canals of Venice or the plains of the Midwest; but no matter what wonderful place she imagined, she always awoke to the rolling hills of Georgia—her safe place.

With the wind dying down she could hear the horses

neighing, acting like barking dogs, wanting her to throw the next ball. Rolling to her side she watched Bay prancing back and forth along the white center-flex fence that she and her father had built. He limped with every other step. Bay was a well-built gelding that measured just over sixteen hands tall, and his mane and tail waved with every cut he made to catch Madi's attention. They had only been a team for five years but had won many rodeos and bonded as best friends. Madi's father, James Hamlin, often said that Bay was two ax handles wide, and one of the best barrel horses in the Southeast; it was just too bad he couldn't take him out to round up their cattle.

Madi smiled at Bay and rolled back over in time to glimpse a flocculent turtle as it faded into two goldfish. *What a beautiful day for clouds. It must be going to rain this evening with them being so fluffy.* In the distance she could hear Ally laughing as she swung higher and higher in the tire swing tied to the large oak in the front yard. Ally, Madi's only child, had just turned eight and was following in her mom's footsteps to become a competitive barrel racer.

The sound of Ally giggling as she stretched out on the swing brought Madi another smile. She could picture Ally's dark brown hair dragging the worn-out spot below the swing. Spring had come early, and the warm weather was welcomed in the Southern states. With the next blink, Madi thought about the last two years and all the unexpected change they brought, starting with the ten months from hell.

It only seemed like yesterday that she was pacing the third floor of Emory Hospital with her cell phone glued to her ear. Five rooms down from her tense conversation were her daughter and husband. Cole, her husband of nine years, had been in a coma for close to ten months following a freak accident with a tractor and baler. His love was farming, and with the help of Madi's father, he had become one of the more successful hay growers in the state of Georgia. One day he had been untangling a hay line that was caught around the power takeoff shaft that led from the hay baler to the tractor. Nobody knew for sure, but they speculated he pulled the line while the tractor was in gear, snatching him violently down on top of the baler where he struck his head. They had found him later that night after he didn't come in from the fields. He had been unconscious ever since.

James, Madi's father, had inherited Hamlin Farms from his father who had started growing hay during the Great Depression. Mr. Hamlin was a Southern farmer who believed in seeking God's will, whether in his marriage or his hay crops. He rested and burned the land every seven years, claiming it was God's decision and not his. Many of their regular customers would argue with him, but he stood strong to his word. James believed it was his father's devout proclamation that gave their hay a strong protein content, and the farmers the best nutrients for their livestock.

Cole had grown up in Waynesboro, Georgia, just five miles from Hamlin Farms, and married his high school sweetheart, Madi. She was seldom seen without her horse when she was home, and at an early age she became a competitive barrel racer and put her name in the record books. Her parents pushed her to go to college and become a veterinarian or specialize in equine science, but she was adamant about chasing the rodeo dream. Leaving home at the age of eighteen, she joined the professional circuit and spent her time on the roads between Arizona and Georgia, while Cole played football for Georgia Tech. Both proved to be auspicious in their goals, and with Cole entering the draft and Madi competing in the NRA finals in Las Vegas, it seemed nothing would hinder them.

But an early knee injury sidelined Cole; and seeing his dreams fade, Madi choose to stay home at his side. After a year off of football, he fell in love with farming and begged Madi to continue chasing her dream of returning to the road. Cole never missed a rodeo and cheered her on from the bottom row of every arena she ran. Madi was committed to winning the finals, and even during her pregnancy and the birth of their daughter, she only took off four months.

At the age of thirty-one, she could only watch and pray as her high school sweetheart—father to her six-year-old daughter, and husband of nine years—fought for his life in room 308.

Chapter 2

After a long battle, Cole's body began shutting down; and on a chilly spring day, Cole left behind his little girl and the love of his life. A few rainy days later, at two o'clock in the afternoon, they put him to rest in the Waynesboro cemetery. The weeks to follow were a blur, and Madi knew she had to compete and get back on the road to keep her mind sane. But she found herself struggling, missing the man in the front row who had always hollered her name.

Now, as she lay in the field, Madi thought how life hadn't at all turned out like she'd hoped. It hadn't even been a week since Bay injured himself coming down an alleyway in an outdoor arena in East Texas. She had barely placed at any rodeos in the last two years. Maybe everyone was right; she had lost her confidence. Maybe she should quit rodeo.

"Hey, kiddo," a raspy voice said.

She looked up, and a straw hat in her view blocked the sunlight from her eyes. "Hey, Dad."

"These old knees don't always work right," he said, struggling to take a seat in the grass beside her. She smiled at his persistence to join her. "That little girl is just like her mother," he said, looking toward Ally as she tangled herself up in the swing.

"She's tougher than her mom," Madi replied.

"Oh, I don't know about that. You've got a lot of fight left in you."

"I sure don't feel it," she said.

"What did the vet say about Bay?" Her dad pointed to the horse who had finally settled into grazing.

"Two, maybe three months of staying off him," she answered.

James did his best to spin around and point at another pasture. "What about Grey? He seems to be ready. He placed in the last few shows you took him to."

"I don't think he's ready for the big show. He still takes one too many strides on the third barrel. Plus he just doesn't have Bay's speed."

"Honey, I don't know of *any* horses as fast as Bay." He chuckled. Bay threw his head up in their direction as though he heard them talking about him.

"I don't know, Dad, I just don't have it anymore." Tears began to fill her green eyes and she made no attempt to hide them from her dad.

Leaning over, he said, "Well, I have a suggestion. Your mother didn't like it at first but I think it will help."

"What's that?" she answered, wiping her face.

"An old friend of mine has a cottage on Wilkes Key in Florida, and he's not using it this summer. Why don't you take half-pint over there and y'all disappear for three months? By then Bay will be healed and you can make that decision then."

"I can't just pack up and leave for three months!"

"Why? What's keeping you here? Sweetheart, two years is too long to mourn."

"I'm not mourning! I'm not going crazy and all the other things people are saying!" she exclaimed, standing to her feet.

"Nobody's saying those things," James said. He struggled to his knees.

Pulling him up, Madi stared her father in the eyes. "I've let him go."

"No, kiddo. You haven't."

Madi took a deep breath and walked slowly toward the house.

James shook his head, agreeing with his own words. Looking back at the sunlight that glistened off the field, he thought, *This place has always kept a magical feel. I wish it would speak to my little girl.* He watched as a gust of wind blew through the grass and caused it to ripple like water, consecutive waves passing around him and catching up to Madi before she made it to the fence.

She placed her hands on the top rung but stopped shy of climbing over the white PVC rails. Lowering her head she took a deep breath in through her nose and exhaled. "I'll think about it," she replied without turning.

"Thank you," he replied with a hint of a smile. With one last glance toward the field, he began following her to the house.

"Hey, Fred!" he shouted at Ally. Cole had given her that nickname. No one was really sure where he picked it up, but it seemed to fit her.

Her head popped up. "What's up, Grandpa?"

"Let's see how high we can get you in that swing," he replied.

After stepping onto the porch, Madi watched for a brief moment as her ailing father pushed her free-spirited daughter in the very tire swing he once pushed her. She could smell the chicken frying in the black kettle pot her mom had used for years.

"Madi, help me open this can," her mother said from inside the screen door.

Madi walked into the kitchen; it hadn't been updated since her high school days—same old white countertops with silver trim, and more picture of roosters than they had outside. Rena was a faithful wife and mother, never losing her temper and always saying something positive no matter the situation. Handprints of flour lined her apron and matched her graying hair, but her complexion was still youthful even in her aging years.

"Mom, did Dad tell you about this cottage idea?" she asked.

"He did."

"And what do you think?" Her mother put down the paper bag of flour she used for flouring the chicken.

"I think it's a good idea. Get away for a while. And if you don't like it, just come home." She gave Madi a smile and picked the sack back up.

Madi thought for a moment; her mom always had good advice and always kept it simple. *If it doesn't work, just come back.* "Do you think there are any kids there for Ally?"

"I'm sure there are. Alicia makes friends with everyone," her mother cheerily answered.

Madi smiled and sat down after fixing a glass of sweet tea. *My sweet little Alicia.* Cole had picked out that name, and everyone knew where he got it from—the hay fields of Alicia.

Chapter 3

Standing in his third-story apartment overlooking Central Park in Manhattan, Michael Curry finished his bottle of water and looked at his newest concert promotion poster. He glanced back out at the transcendent view of the park and tried to grasp the idea of a "Night with Michael Curry." *Sounds more like a gigolo ad.* He walked toward his couch and placed the poster on his black lacquered baby grand piano, one of his most loved and prized possessions. When he paused for a moment at a huge floor-to-ceiling mirror, the image of a six-foot-two, dark-haired man reflected back, and he furrowed his forehead. *I need to start working out more!*

Michael's apartment was set in a modern-meets-rustic fashion with oval doorways and cobblestone walls. The fireplace was dressed in black marble with only one large piece of framed art on the mantel—a musical note drawn on cream-colored paper with black pencil. His longtime friend Muturi Okar, an African composer, had drawn the picture while they were on tour in Northern Europe.

Hearing a buzzing coming from the kitchen, he walked in to see a text on his phone. "What did you think of the poster?" the text read.

"I don't know yet," he responded to his manager. Robin Abbott was not only his manager but also a friend and mother figure since she had discovered him in an orphanage. Michael, then a teenager, had been playing for an orphanage benefit when Robin and her husband first heard him play. They were more astonished that he had taught himself to play than at the piece he had written for that evening, but they soon adopted him and supported his blossoming talent.

He didn't really remember anything from his early childhood; he only knew he was abandoned as an infant. In the Catholic orphanage, he grew up playing the piano and allowing his talents to take his imagination other places. Blessed as an athlete, he loved playing baseball with his friends and was always looking for a pickup game of basketball. But his true love was music.

Now, years later, Michael was a successful composer who financially supported the orphanage of his childhood and regularly returned to teach piano lessons and mentor other children. The most powerful words he ever heard had come from a volunteer baseball coach who had told him, "I'm proud of you." The words were etched into his memory, and he repeated them often to the young children who only knew of the orphanage as their home.

The music of one of his uncut pieces sounded from his phone; he picked it up and answered the call. "What do you mean I don't know?" Robin asked.

"It sounds like a date with me," he replied.

"Well, it is! If you don't like it we can keep trying; we are not in a hurry. How's the writing coming?"

"Slow! I can't wrap my head around this album," he said.

"Okay, just breathe." Michael had heard Robin say that a million times. "Come over tonight and eat with Doug and I. When was the last time you got a home-cooked meal?" she added.

"It's been awhile."

"Good. Seven o'clock and bring a red," she insisted.

Doug and Robin had asked Michael to come live with them

when he was sixteen. Not long after that, another musician asked Michael to open for his shows; and with Robin acting as manager, Michael's career took off. Michael spent most of his time with Doug when Robin handled his shows. They had built a strong relationship over the years.

Doug had been paralyzed for close to thirty years, having been injured in a training exercise with the Marine Corps in San Diego. After recovering he served as an assistant to a navel general who had lost his wife and children in a car accident. Years later and after a close friendship, the general passed away and left his inheritance to Doug. Since Doug didn't have any children of his own, he was happy to form a fatherly bond with Michael.

A red? He searched through his wine cabinet and found a Spanish blend that Doug favored. *Buenos Tiempos. Good times! After the whole bottle, that might be true.* Looking at his Movado watch, he saw he didn't have much time to make it to Doug and Robin's house. He quickly changed into slacks and a button-down black shirt. Snatching his jacket and scarf and the bottle from the counter, he dashed through the door toward the stairs. He reached the foyer with marble floors and heard Henry, an older man who tended the door. "Mr. Curry, you're looking sharp tonight. Big date?" Henry smiled.

"Dinner with the Abbotts," he replied.

"Man sakes alive. Mr. Abbott is a good man. Did I ever tell you about him giving me those nice Italian shoes?"

"I think you did," Michael replied, having heard the story well over a dozen times. He liked Henry; he didn't know if it was his jolly nature or his honesty, but he always had a big smile on his face.

"Now, before I get you a car, you got to answer me one question," Henry started.

"I'll find her in due time. No rushing," Michael answered. It was the same question every week for the last year about Michael finding that right person.

Henry started laughing. "You go on away from here, Mr. Curry. You is funny people." Still laughing, he waved at a black town car.

Michael wrapped his scarf around his neck and stepped out into the cold air of New York. Climbing into the car, he smiled. "Thanks, Henry. Long Island, please," he told the driver.

A short drive later, Michael started up the steps to the house. Before reaching the top, the door swung open and Robin stood in the opening. "I'm glad you're here," she said, hugging him.

"I got this for Doug." He showed the bottle to her.

"Oh, he'll like that."

Michael closed the wooden door behind him and followed Robin into the dining room. "I hope you like this one," he said to Doug.

"Let me see what you have there," Doug said, bringing his wheelchair around the table. "Get the opener. I bet I do like this one."

Chapter 4

With her new bathing suit on, Ally scampered past Madi. "Slow down before you run someone over," Madi said. Putting her glass in the sink, Madi turned to find her dad walking into the kitchen.

"Just got off the phone with the Lawrences, and everything is set with the cottage," he said.

"I have to admit, it's going to be nice to just get away."

"Well, there's a catch to using the cottage," James said with a smirk.

Madi rolled her eyes. "What's the catch?"

"He is taking his wife to Europe for about the same time, and he wanted to know if you would take care of their parrot, Augustus."

"You're kidding?" she asked.

"A parrot!" Ally exclaimed.

James reached down and picked her up. "Yes, a big red-lored Amazon that happens to be green."

A big smile formed across her face, then she glanced at her mom. "This is going to be so cool."

Madi didn't reply. She knew there was no winning. Now she was babysitting a bird. "All right, kiddo, go change your clothes," Madi said as James set her on the linoleum floor. Ally sprinted toward her room, losing a flip-flop en route. "I better go feed before the sun sets," Madi said, slipping into her boots.

Walking out onto the wraparound porch, she could see the sun beginning to touch the farthest pasture. Their three barns all faced the house, with the middle barn for her barrel horses. The barns lined the white PVC fence and after a major storm last year, each one had a new red tin roof.

"Y'all come on!" Madi shouted toward the pastures. Before she could get the words out, each horse broke into a dead run toward the barn. Bay brought up the rear with his head down, limping on his right front leg.

Madi pushed the sliding tin door open, exposing the hall of the barn. Walking through the hall she opened each stall door before reaching the back gate, where five horses waited impatiently. Opening the gate she stepped out of the way and let them run to their stalls.

Bay just made it to the gate. "Hey, fella." Madi put her arm around his neck; she could tell he was hurting. "I'll get you some medicine," she said and walked toward the feed room. Once everyone got a scoop of sweet feed and a scoop of oats, she made her way back to Bay's stall. Leaning over the gate and running her fingers through his mane, she said, "Bay, me and half-pint are going to take off for a few months. I'm going to let you have your rest and I'm going to get some too. I'll come back and check on you." Bay nudged the hanging bucket with a mouth full of oats, his broad eyes cut in Madi's direction. *Daddy always said horses with big eyes could be trusted.*

She slid down Bay's stall door and sat on the concrete floor as tears started welling up. *Why did you have to leave? I miss you so much.*

Heartbroken and unable to hide it any longer, she lowered her head into her knees and began sobbing uncontrollably.

"Robin, you still amaze me with your cooking," Michael said as he cleared the table.

"Go visit with Doug and I'll finish here," she said.

Michael walked into the living room where Doug was opening a bottle of brandy. "Grab that box and let's retire to the veranda," Doug said.

Michael picked up the wooden box of Cubans and followed Doug out into the cold air. Doug pushed himself up to a round stone pit and pushed a red button. At the sound of a click, a fire erupted in the pit. Michael watched the flames dance above the blue marble glass that lined the inside. He was still impressed that even though he was bound to a wheelchair, Doug still had a *savoir vivre* demeanor.

With a flash of a Zippo lighter in his face, Michael was blinded for a moment by the flame as Doug lit his cigar. Then he settled into a deep cushioned chair and propped his feet on the stone pit. In the distance he could see a freighter coming into port, the calm water reflected the luminescent lights lining the rails around the ship. The steam from the stacks reached high into the cold night. *I bet that's a cold ride on that bow,* he thought.

The sliding door shut as Robin joined them with a glass of the Spanish blend left over from supper. She brought a wool blanket with her and laid it across her lap.

"Do you mind sharing?" Doug asked her.

She rolled her eyes. "I just sat down."

Doug reached out for it and before he could pull part of it over his legs, she walked back in to retrieve another blanket for him. Her reaction surprised Michael but he said nothing.

"He insists we sit out here no matter how cold it gets," she said, pulling the door closed.

"Now that's not true. We stayed inside during the last snow shower," Doug laughed.

Michael leaned back against the cushion and blew a puff of smoke into the cold air; he couldn't tell what was smoke and what was breath. In the distance they could hear the horn from the freighter. "That never gets old," Doug replied.

"I could live on the ocean forever," Michael said.

Doug sat up in his chair. "Well, it's funny you make that comment."

Michael gave him a funny look. "What do you mean?"

"Why don't you get out of here for the summer? Go somewhere quiet and write," Doug added.

"I wish."

"Well, your wish is coming true. I have acquired a cottage on an island north of Tampa, Florida, on Wilkes Key. It's a small island, maybe ten square miles with a few hundred people on it. Mostly retired. Take off and go write, clear your head."

"That sounds nice but I have a lot to do here to prepare for the fall tour," Michael replied.

"You've admitted that you have been struggling. Go. Lord knows we'll never use it," Robin interjected.

Michael knew she was right; he had confided in her last month that he felt he was in a slump. Nothing was coming to him and every time he sat at the piano, he seemed to be playing the same old music he composed years ago. He knew it was time to do something to bring back his flair.

"What's this cottage look like?" he asked.

"It's a two bedroom with a screened-in back porch that faces the gulf," Robin quickly said with anticipation of his decision. "We'll have your piano delivered for you," she added.

Michael took a long drag on the Cuban and tilted his head back, blowing the smoke up. "No . . . ," he started. "I want a simple piano. I want to try something different. Maybe it will spark something," he said, blowing more smoke into the air.

Chapter 5

The silver Jeep Grand Cherokee sped down the interstate with bags in the back and a box of candy Hot Tamales in the cup holder. “Look, sweetie, we’re crossing into Florida,” Madi said, pointing out her windshield at the state line sign.

A big smile formed across Ally’s face. “How much farther?”

“We still have a few more hours,” Madi said, knowing that she would lose the smile on Ally’s face. She scrolled the satellite radio to a kids’ channel in hopes of something to cheer her up. They had left earlier that morning with the goal to be at the cottage by midafternoon. Madi was glad it wasn’t far.

“Do you want to play I Spy?” she asked Ally.

“No. Tell me about the parrot.”

“Well, he’s about this big.” She held her hands about eight inches apart. “And his name is Augustus,” she added.

Ally looked puzzled. “Augustus?”

“Yep, that’s what they said. He’s named after a movie cowboy.”

Ally tried to say it again. “Augus . . . Agus . . . I’m just going to call him Gus.”

A few hours later, the Jeep Grand Cherokee pulled off the interstate and into a gas station. “Let’s fill up and stretch our legs.” Madi smiled at Ally.

“How much more, Mom?”

"Under an hour. And before long we'll get to smell the ocean," she said with excitement.

After filling up and replenishing their waters and candy Swedish Fish, the two girls pulled out onto Highway 24.

ൟ

A black ML450 Mercedes waited for a silver Jeep Grand Cherokee to pull out onto the highway to allow room to pull into the gas station.

Parking at the pump and stepping out of the ML450, Michael stretched his arms above his head. *One hour left!*

ൟ

Madi barely had put the Jeep in park before Ally bolted from the passenger seat toward the beach. Their cottage was across the street from the gulf and just down from the beach access. Ally cut through the neighbor's yard across the street, Madi hot on her heels. She ran halfway onto the beach and turned with a huge smile from ear to ear toward her mother.

"Ally, we can't just run through someone's yard! You see that path down there?" she said, pointing.

"Yes, ma'am."

"That's how we get to the beach. Okay?" Madi said. She wasn't sure Ally even heard her; she was already on her knees, digging in the sand.

Madi made her way down to the water. It was a calm day and the emerald waters glistened with the sun beaming down. She took a deep breath and exhaled, stretching her arms above her head. Bending down she ran her hand through the ripples of water and felt the coolness of the late spring in it.

Something caught her attention out of the corner of her eye. "Ally, look! Dolphins!" Ally quickly joined her and held onto

Madi's leg; she didn't say anything, but Madi could feel Ally's heart pounding with excitement.

"Come here." Reaching down, she picked Ally up and held her. "This is going to be the greatest vacation." She thought this would probably be the last year she would be able to pick her up, too. They sat down and watched the dolphins play just off the beach, and they could see a baby trying to jump but only coming halfway out of the water.

"Mom!" Ally suddenly said with so much excitement she scared Madi. "We have to go meet Gus!" And she was off again, taking the beach path to cut back to their cottage.

I hope this bird doesn't bite, she thought, chasing after her daughter.

Reaching the front yard she stopped momentarily to observe the cottage. The tan siding with green louvered shutters was a cute touch. It had a brown tin roof and was lined with palms and azaleas, and the St. Augustine grass had been freshly cut. *Thank goodness I don't have to mow grass this summer!*

"Mom! Come see!" She heard Ally from inside the opened front door. When she walked in she was relieved to see Gus shaking Ally's finger. "He shakes!" Ally said, still burning with excitement.

"Well hello, Mr. Gus," Madi said. Gus squawked back. Both girls stared at each other, then broke into a hysterical laugh. Before they realized it Gus was laughing with them in a human voice, and they laughed even harder, filling the cottage with much-needed joy.

Ally picked up a forked stick with two ends. "What's this for?" Before Madi could answer, Gus leaped out of his cage and onto the stick. "Oh my gosh!" Ally exclaimed. Gus perked up on the stick as if he were going to lead the way.

Madi quickly made her way over to the front door. "Now, Gus stays inside and the doors stay shut. Last thing we need is to lose their bird," Madi confirmed with Ally. Again she wasn't sure Ally had heard; she was too busy walking her new friend around the cottage.

In the meantime, Madi took some time to familiarize herself with the two-bedroom cottage. The kitchen opened into the living room with a bar and four bar stools tucked under the overhang. In the kitchen, dark cherry cabinets with under-cabinet lighting hung above granite countertops with a round, smooth edge. She peeked out in the backyard to see a bench swing under a weeping willow; the area was small but cozy. Walking through the beach-themed living room, she headed into the master bedroom where the beach theme continued with tiled floors and light blue paint.

Ally walked in the smaller bedroom with Gus still hanging onto the edge of the stick. "Is this my room?"

"Yes, you'll be just across from my room," Madi assured her.

Since Cole's death, Ally had trouble sleeping because of nightmares and spent many nights in bed with her mom.

"Can we move Gus's cage in here?" she asked, with puppy dog eyes.

"No, he is probably more comfortable in the living room," Madi said, thinking that those sleeping problems might have just disappeared with a parrot in the picture now.

"Put him back in his cage and let's go get our bags from the Jeep," Madi said, scooting Ally and the bird toward the living room. She picked her keys up from the table beside the front door and pushed the trunk button for the Jeep's back door to open.

After pulling their bags out, she walked toward the passenger side and found Ally picking up a spilled box of Hot Tamales. "Don't eat the ones on the ground," she said, taking the box from her.

"Ten-second rule," Ally responded with a grin.

Lugging their bags to the cottage, Madi realized there were two rocking chairs on the front porch. *Those will be nice.* She wondered if she could see the sun setting from that view; maybe she would be able to see it disappear into the ocean. Looking down the narrow road, she saw a couple of other cottages, each with different colors and architecture.

Opening the door she found Ally with Gus again. "Ally, you can have all the time in the world with Gus. I need help right now."

"But he likes his neck scratched," she replied. Gus was bent so far over that he looked as if he was about to fall off his cage; his head buried downward and his feathers ruffled as he enjoyed his neck massage. Madi smiled. It was the first time in a while that Ally looked at peace. *Thanks, Dad. You are always right.*

Just then Madi noticed the neighbors pulling in across the street. She waved but wasn't sure they waved back through the tinted windows. She watched the brake lights go off as the Mercedes ML450 came to a complete stop in the drive.

Chapter 6

Standing in the yard stretching, Michael observed the house. It was painted in a low tone of yellow with the trim a tranquil blue. The louvered shutters on the front door matched the trim along with the Bahama-style shutters on the windows. Walking in he noticed that the shutters depleted the sunlight in the house. *I might have to take those down.* The inside was designed in a rustic beach theme with wooden floors. Michael thought wood was an odd flooring choice to have near the beach. Walking out into the screened back porch, he found his Stearns baby grand piano. *So much for staying simple.*

He sat down and played a few chords from his latest album. *Man, that sounds good!* He stood, then walked to the opening and gazed out at the surf. The warm wind pierced the screen and blew against his face. He watched an elderly couple walk along the water holding hands as a dachshund puppy jumped in and out of the ocean. He took his phone out of his pocket and texted Robin: "Finally here."

Opening the refrigerator he saw two bottles of white and a fruit basket with a note. Opening the envelope he read, "Enjoy the summer and rest!" He smiled at the fruit basket from Doug. As he munched on a slice of apple, he went back to his car to retrieve the rest of his bags, leaving the front door open. Walking back in with a stack of sheet music, he thought he heard something run through the hall. He peeked around the corner and down the hall but saw nothing out of the ordinary. Turning to set the music down on the bar, he was confronted with a yelping bark. *Holy crap!* He lost his footing and both arms shot up in reaction. As the sheet music rained down he looked to find the same small dachshund sitting in front of him—still wet and sandy from the beach.

It bolted back down the hall and Michael chased him to the entry of the hall. Bending to one knee, he said, "Come here, boy!" He coaxed the puppy in a high voice while wincing about the paw prints on the freshly polished floors. The little guy tucked his tail between his legs and sheepishly made his way to Michael. Once Michael began to pet him, the dog relieved himself out of excitement.

"What the . . . " Michael said, jetting toward the kitchen for paper towels. The little dog ran through his own pee and tracked it to the kitchen as he chased Michael. "This isn't a game!" Michael said, picking him up. But to his surprise, the little guy got excited again, this time relieving himself on Michael.

"Holy crap!" Michael hollered. Holding the little pup with one hand, Michael began spraying everything he pointed the dachshund at. "How do you stop the darn thing!?" Running to the bathroom for a towel and still carrying the dog, he unknowingly left a spray trail of pee across the couch, end table, rug, and everything else in the path toward the bathroom. Panicking, Michael did the only thing he knew to do—pushed a large bath towel between the little legs of his newly acquired friend.

Michael, his mouth cocked sideways with disgust, stood beside the tub holding the squirmy wet dog. A loud knock at the back door interrupted his thoughts of revenge. "Just a second," he shouted back. He grabbed another towel and wiped his shirt and carried the leaking dog in the other.

An elderly lady stood outside the screen porch. "Oh, you found Amos!" she said out of excitement.

"If you're referring to this nonstop peeing animal, then yes, I found him."

"Oh, come to mama," she said with hands held wide.

"That's why I call him peepee dog," a scruffy voice said from behind her. The man wore a Hawaiian shirt and blue shorts with black socks and loafers. He tilted the lens on his sunglasses and smiled at Michael.

"I'm sorry, Amos doesn't know a stranger. I hope he wasn't trouble for you," the lady said.

Michael looked back at his pee-drenched living room and kitchen. "No, he wasn't any trouble."

"Oh, what a beautiful piano," she exclaimed, pushing Michael to the side while inviting herself in. She looked back at him. "Do you play?" she asked.

Michael stood dumbfounded at the question. "Yes, I do," he replied.

"Play us something," the lady insisted.

"Maybe some other time; I have to finish unpacking," he answered, trying not to be rude. His type-A personality was setting in and he was not handling the pee situation well.

"Come on, dear, you found the mutt. Let this young man get back to his business," the elderly man said, insinuating he knew his wife was pushy.

Not taking the hint she turned to Michael. "Are you married? Do you have kids?" she asked.

What's next? he thought. But Michael was respectful and said, "No ma'am, I am single with no kids." She began to say something. "And no, I've never been married," he interrupted.

She gave him a big smile. "There's a beautiful young lady who just moved in across the street. You should go introduce yourself," she replied.

"Stop being a matchmaker, Helen!" the older man said. He reached into the porch and pulled the lady and the dog outside with him. "I'm Otis Wellman, and this is Helen . . . the date doctor," he sarcastically said toward his wife. "We live three doors down. Let me know if anything breaks," he added.

"Breaks?" Michael asked.

"Otis is the island handyman," Helen quickly answered.

"Well, I'll keep that in mind, but right now I need a flood relief team," he said. The Wellmans gave him a confusing look, not realizing the welcome peepee dog had left.

"Since you and Amos are new friends, you can keep him anytime," Helen said.

Michael's eyes widened in horror. "Okay, I'll keep that in mind."

As they walked off, he heard her ask Otis, "Do you think he's gay? No girlfriends!"

Michael wasn't sure whether to laugh or pack up and head back to New York.

ᘓᘔ

Madi rolled over and put her arm around Ally, who was sound asleep with her favorite stuffed bear under her arms. She smiled at the peace she was starting to feel. While drifting off to sleep, she thought for a moment she heard the sounds of a piano in the light, warm breeze that entered her bedroom through the open window.

Chapter 7

Michael opened the one-car garage to find a four-seater golf cart hooked up to a charger. He saw the keys dangling from the starter and admired the chrome rims and candy apple red paint. *Well, I guess I can park the car for the summer and ride in this.* He slipped into his flip-flops and jumped in the cart to head to the grocery store.

The small store was located in the downtown part of the island. It was old and matched most of the other buildings with its wraparound porches both upstairs and down. The doorbell chimed as the door slammed behind him. He instantly loved the old wooden floors and wooden shelves that lined the store with stocked groceries and bread. Grabbing a basket, he walked to the far side of the store and found an assortment of fresh fruit and vegetables. He loaded up on celery and kale for his normal morning juice, then noticed the man behind the counter staring at him.

"Good morning," Michael said.

"Are you the young man staying in the cottage with the piano on the back porch?" the man asked.

"Yes, sir, how did you know that?" Michael asked.

"Those boys stopped by here lost as a goose in a snowstorm," the man replied.

Michael wasn't sure what he was talking about. "Goose?"

"The boys that delivered it. I gave 'em directions and a Coke. They seemed frustrated."

"Well, thank you. I owe you," Michael said.

"Nah. So whatcha doing with the piano?"

Michael thought for a moment. *People are sure curious here.* "I write music. Figured it would be nice to spend the summer here writing."

"Well, you picked a good place. Let me know if there is something you need. If you don't see it, I'll order it." And he went back to unpacking a box of fresh oranges.

Michael strolled through the store and gathered the remaining things on his list.

"So did you find everything?" the man asked.

"Yes, thank you. How did you know I was the one with the piano?" Michael asked.

"The delivery guys said they were delivering the piano to a young guy. Not many single thirty-something-year-olds on this island. Matter of fact, not many forty- or fifty-year-old guys either."

Michael watched as the man finished bagging the remaining groceries, thinking that this must be the main link to the island gossip. He still hadn't been to the barber or to Randy's Bar and Grill yet.

Gathering his two paper bags of fruit and other items, he walked to the screen door. Reaching it just in time, he held it open with his back, allowing a young blonde to enter. *Wow!*

"Thank you." She smiled. She had shoulder-length hair and a petite figure. For a moment they awkwardly looked at each other. *Ok, where is this going?* Michael thought to himself. But his thoughts were interrupted by the springy little brown-haired girl who seemed to come out of nowhere. She gave him a big smile. "Hi! I'm Ally!" she said without missing a beat to her skip.

"Well, good morning. My name is Michael." He smiled as she stuck her hand out to shake.

"I'm sorry, she doesn't know a stranger," the woman said, guiding Ally into the store.

"It's okay. It's nice to get a cheerful greeting," Michael replied as the two of them disappeared into the store.

As Michael put the two sacks in the golf cart he heard Ally from inside the store. "He's driving the red golf cart. Can I go ride?" Not hearing her mother's answer, Michael smiled at the innocence of the child.

Driving back to the cottage he passed an older couple jogging. The man wore his red, white, and blue headband, short shorts, and tube socks with white running shoes. The woman was moderately dressed in aerobic pants and a blue shirt. Both waved as Michael passed. *I really need to get in better shape!*

Just as soon as he'd had the thought, he drove past another building whose sign read The Island Gym. Sliding to a stop and holding his bags, he spun the cart around and parked in front of the white columned porch. As he entered he saw the open space sufficiently filled with state-of-the-art equipment. *Wow, this is nicer than my apartment gym,* he thought.

A young lady walked out of the back. "Hello, can I help you?"

"Yes, I'm only here for three months. Do you offer a membership for that time period? And if so, is there anyone who personally trains here?" he asked.

She smiled. "We have monthly memberships and I am the trainer here."

Michael didn't doubt her ability; she was well built and had the disposition of someone who constantly worked out. "Can I ask how you train?" he hesitantly asked.

"I mostly do resistance and core training. What are you looking for?" she asked.

"That's perfect. When can we start?"

The question stunned her. "Well, today if you'd like. Three times a week?" She looked at her book that seemed to be more full than he expected. "What about two o'clock this afternoon?" she asked.

"Sounds good. My name is Michael."

"Nice to meet you. I'm Deanna."

The diploma on the wall caught Michael's attention on the way out. Master's degree in Health and Exercise from California University of Pennsylvania. *Nice!* Maybe this vacation was just what he needed after all.

Chapter 8

The following day, Michael was so sore he could barely hold his coffee mug. Sipping slowly he heard a loud, low bark from outside his screen door. When he opened the door he found a basset hound sitting outside. "Good morning to you," Michael replied. The hound barked back as if saying hello.

Michael stepped down and began scratching her behind her ears; she quickly rolled over to her back, begging him to scratch her belly. "Well, you are a friendly hound."

After a few minutes, he looked out at the beach, retrieved his sunglasses from the kitchen counter, and headed to the sand. He patted his thigh as he walked past the dog. "Come on!" She stood to her small fat legs and waddled beside him to the water.

They sat down in the sand and he noticed the nametag dangling from her collar. "Lady! That's a beautiful name."

He watched the small waves crash on the desolate beach, as the teal water sparkled in the sun. Michael pulled down his aviators to catch the true color of the water. The steam rolled out of his cup as he blew his coffee—the one thing he was sure the store clerk wouldn't be able to get. A few years ago a friend had turned him onto a coffee company in Nicaragua, and with every bag he ordered, half of the money went toward sending kids to summer camp. Michael loved the idea of helping kids and quickly fell in love with the fresh coffee.

Lady turned and faced him with her back toward the gulf. "You'd rather be scratched than look at this sight?" He smiled at her. While he scratched her head she perked up and looked over his shoulder. Catching her eyes, he began to turn to see who was walking up.

Michael wasn't fully turned when it hit him. Stunned and in shock, he wasn't sure why he was being attacked. He swatted the assailant out of his face but couldn't seem to defend himself. It didn't matter how hard or how fast he swatted—he was losing this battle. Finally gathering his sight back, he saw green feathers floating in front of his face. "What the hell!" he shrieked.

A tired and out-of-breath green parrot stood in the sand facing him. Lady took two steps toward Michael and sat back down. It was apparent she wasn't interested in getting involved in the fight. After all, her new friend just got whipped by a bird. "What is it with this island and animals!? And thanks for defending me," he said, looking over at Lady, who seemed to have a smile on her face with her tongue hanging out.

The same little girl who had introduced herself at the store appeared from around the side of his house. "Gus!" she screamed, running toward the beach.

Michael looked back down at the bird. "Gus?" He could swear that the eight-inch green beast was growling at him.

"I take it that this attack bird belongs to you?" he said, his hair still messed up from the aerial ambush.

"He's not an attack bird, he's Gus," she said, picking him up. Her attention quickly went to Lady. "Is this your dog?"

"No, just a friend," he said.

"Awwww, she's pretty," Ally said, bending down to pet her with bird in hand. Gus quickly struck toward Lady's nose. Taking no chances, Lady backed up two steps; she didn't want anything to do with this colorful vulture.

"Here! Hold Gus." Ally pushed the bird into Michael's arms.

"Wait, I don't think . . . " he started to say, but it was too late. The bird went back into attack mode and Michael dropped the vicious fighter. "I don't think he likes me!"

Ally's attention returned to Gus. "He likes everyone," she replied. *I don't think so . . . and if he keeps this up we're going to find out what parrot tastes like.*

Lady just sat in the sand, avoiding the fiasco.

"Ally!" a voice shouted from behind him. Turning, he came face-to-face with the girl's mother. "I'm so sorry, she left the door open," she replied, out of breath from running on the sand. She was wearing a white T-shirt with a cardigan and khaki shorts. Michael looked down and saw she was barefooted.

"It's okay, but you might want to put a muzzle on the attack bird." He smiled.

She cut her eyes toward Ally. "Gather up Gus and let's leave this gentleman alone."

"Yes, ma'am," Ally sheepishly replied, pulling Gus tighter into her arms.

She turned back to Michael and started to say something, but then pointed toward his shorts. "Are you bleeding?"

Michael looked down at his arms. "No, I don't think so."

"It's your hand," Ally said, pointing to the small bite mark on the back of his right hand. The girl's mother began to blush out of embarrassment.

"Don't worry, it's just a scratch," he said.

"Is this your house?" she asked.

"For the summer."

"Do you have bandages for that cut?"

"I don't know, I just got here," he said, trying to remember if he had seen any medical supplies in the cottage.

"Follow us across the street. The least I can do is bandage you up." She smiled.

Normally Michael would have passed on the invite, but the

last thing he wanted to do was get some strange infection on his hand. “Well, I don’t want to put you out . . .” he started to say.

“Nonsense, come on,” she said, walking toward the path down the beach.

“We’ll cut through my yard. No sense in you guys walking down to the path.”

Ally piped up. “Mom said it’s the right thing to do and not to cut through your yard.”

Michael smiled at the woman, not sure if Ally was innocently repeating her mother’s word or trying to get a free pass. “Well, you and your mother can cut through my yard anytime. How’s that?” he said. Ally gave him a big smile, leaving him to wonder.

Lady took off down the beach. “Where’s your dog going?” Ally asked.

“Lady? I’m not sure. She doesn’t belong to me, just a neighborhood friend. I would guess she’s had all the excitement she wants for one day.”

Michael watched as the girls mother walked lightly across the road without shoes and then across the yard. He paused before entering, “Come on in.” The woman waved him inside.

Walking out of her bathroom, the young woman handed Michael a bandage. “By the way, I’m Madi.” She stuck her hand out.

“I’m Michael.”

“Well, again, I’m sorry for our bird. He really belongs to the people who own this cottage. We’re bird-sitting for the summer and aren’t off to a good start.” She looked at Ally again.

Madi started walking toward the door. Michael wanted to ask more questions but felt it wasn’t the right time. Plus, with them living across the street, there would be plenty of time to get to know his new neighbors.

“Don’t worry. Anytime I can be of assistance for catching birds, maybe next time I can wear one of those attack dog outfits,” he said, smiling at Ally. She laughed. “If you need anything just let me know,” he said to Madi.

"Thanks." She watched him cross the street.

Fighting the urge to turn around, Michael kept walking. *Man, she's beautiful!*

Chapter 9

Michael was still invigorated after the crazy morning, and for the first time he sat down at the piano with something in mind. An inspiration had struck him earlier—before the parrot had attacked him—and with it still fresh he proceeded with his usual ritual. He closed his eyes and without pressing the keys he ran his hands over them; they were cold and smooth and felt new to him. Listening only to his breath, the waves that crashed on the beach caught his attention. The wind had picked up and waves rolled over the white sand in unison. He opened his eyes and could feel himself unsettled. Getting up he turned off all the lights, except for one floor lamp on the back porch.

Now back on the bench he felt his mind drifting to the inspiration that he experienced earlier. Before he realized it, his hands were moving over the keys, this time striking several notes. He picked up the tempo to match the waves crashing just outside his door. Moving back and forth in a trance, he imaged himself in a dream with every note as familiar as the last. After a few minutes of steadily playing, he opened his eyes. "I got it!"

He stood up and grabbed paper and a pencil from under the cover of the black leather piano bench. He played a moment, then scribbled something down, and played and scribbled back and forth late into the night.

ꕥ

The next morning Madi walked out onto the front porch to catch the sun rising above the trees down the street. Facing the sandy street, she sat in one of the rocking chairs with her travel mug of coffee and took a deep breath. *Nothing to do today . . . or tomorrow. No stress.* She sat quietly, listening to the waves on the beach behind Michael's cottage. A warm breeze had picked up, fighting off the cool night air.

An elderly couple jogged past and waved. Madi returned the wave, giggling under her breath at the man's red, white, and blue headband. *I need to be running, too.* The air was waking up with seagulls and the sound of a lawn mower in the distance. She closed her eyes and visualized the farm; before she knew it she was back in the fields of Alicia Bermuda.

The clouds swirled and danced in place, forming anything Madi imagined. She could feel herself reaching out and parting the white fluff that formed in the atmosphere. Feeling something nudging her head, she tilted back to see Bay's whiskers in her face. Running her hand over his nose, she could feel his breath. He walked around her and grazed on the grass. She propped her head up and glanced across the field, where the wind moved the grass like water on the open sea.

Hearing a familiar voice, she paused and listened closer—it was Cole! She stood up and looked around but couldn't find him; a strong warm wind engulfed her, she felt his presence. Lying back down she closed her eyes, knowing if she opened them he'd be gone. She could feel his fingers running through her hair. "I miss you!" she repeated with tears rolling off her cheeks. She listened again, and this time hearing his words clearly, she felt at peace.

"Mom?" the soft voice said. Something touched her hand.

She opened her eyes and found Ally standing in front of her. "Well, good morning, sweetheart." She placed her coffee on the floor and picked up the little girl who was still in her nightgown.

Ally noticed the tears on her mother's face but wasn't surprised; it was a familiar sight for the last two years. "I dreamed about home," Ally said, laying her head on Madi's chest.

"Tell me about it."

"I was playing in the field and Bay was with me," she started.

Madi's chest tightened at the voice of her innocent little girl who had already experienced so much loss.

Ally looked up into her mother's damp eyes. "I heard Daddy. I didn't see him but I heard him."

"What did he say?" Madi asked in a soft voice.

Ally motioned for her mother to lean over so she could whisper in her ear. Madi's eyes grew wide and then teared back up; they were the same words she had just heard in her imagination.

"Do you think Daddy is watching over us?" Ally asked.

Madi pulled Ally's little head against her body. "Yes, sweetie, I assure you he's watching over us."

Michael loaded his juicer with the fresh vegetables from the store. His mornings were habitual by nature, and between the juice loaded with vitamins and his coffee loaded with caffeine, it was the only way he could energize his day. After pouring a glass with the thick, green juice, he made his way to the front window. He saw Madi and Ally sitting in their rocking chair. *She's a pretty girl. I wonder what her story is.*

Just then, a howling bark came from his back door. Investigating, he found Lady sitting in the same spot. "Nine o'clock. Is this the time I should expect you every morning?" Lady just looked at him. He opened the door and said, "Well, come on in. Let's see if there's anything here you're interested in."

Chapter 10

Robin hung up the phone.

"Who was that?" Doug asked.

She removed her glasses. "It was a new promoter who wants to expand Michael's tour and possibly start it earlier," she replied.

"He hasn't finished or maybe even started this new album you guys are pushing," Doug said.

"I know exactly what I'm doing. This is unlike anything I've ever seen, but you know how hard Michael pushes himself."

"Well, he is a miracle worker when it comes to music. But he doesn't need any more pushing," Doug said.

"As long as nothing gets in his way again," she said under her breath.

Digging a deeper hole to find moist sand, Ally slapped a handful on her half-made castle. Madi watched from under her umbrella with her earbuds buried in her ears, listening to her favorite alternative station. She closed her eyes and laid her head back against the plastic Adirondack chair she had drug out onto the beach. Her fedora hat rested over her face. Ally walked to the water and gathered a bucket full of salt water. Walking back to her castle, she heard the soft chords of a baby grand piano coming from Michael's house.

She stood and listened to the music wafting from the back porch, then made her way to the cottage. Walking slow and trying her best to catch a peek at who was playing the piano, she ducked behind a palm tree just a few feet from the back porch. Michael's eyes were closed; he was absorbed in the new piece he had started the night before.

When a loud bark came from underneath his piano, Michael shook with the initial shock of the interrupted noise. Opening his eyes and looking under the baby grand, he said, "Now, you can't hang here if you're going to be loud." Lady bowed her head and lay back down.

Ally perked up at the familiar voice coming from inside the screen porch and made a few more steps toward the door with a little more confidence. Lady caught her movement and quickly sat back up with another howling bark.

"Ok, you're going to have to go," Michael said as he stood up.

"Don't make her leave. It's my fault," a little voice said just outside the door.

Michael walked around the piano to find Ally standing innocently on the first step.

"Well, hello, neighbor," Michael said.

"That was really beautiful. Can I listen?" Ally asked.

"Of course you can." Michael looked over her at the yellow umbrella with a head sticking above the Adirondack chair. Opening the screen door. "What do you like?" he asked.

"I don't know," she said walking in.

Michael pulled up a seat for Ally next to his leather bench. He began playing a soft melody and led into one of his top charted pieces. A quarter of the way through it he looked down at the little brown-haired girl sitting beside him; she swayed back and forth with her eyes closed. Lady placed her head in Ally's lap, and Ally opened her eyes long enough to find Lady's ears to scratch.

After the piece he leaned down and asked his new fan, “Well, what did you think?”

“That was absolutely beautiful,” a voice from the screen door replied.

Michael looked to find Madi at the door. “You are welcome to join us.”

“Ally, you can’t be wandering off,” she replied opening the door.

“I’m sorry,” Ally said in a soft voice.

“I am sorry too. I didn’t realize she wandered off without telling you.”

“It’s okay.” She smiled at Michael. “So this is obviously more than a hobby,” she added, looking at the piano.

He smiled knowing that she didn’t know who he was. “Yes, I make a living playing,” he said modestly. “Have a seat and let’s see if I can play something you would like.” Michael motioned to a crate on the floor. She sat beside Ally and wrapped her arm around her, smiling in excitement for their private concert.

He played a pop song, and only a few chords into it, both girls picked up on the tune. Halfway through the song he heard both girls mumbling the words as they swayed back and forth, Madi still smiling. “That’s fun,” she replied after he finished.

“Okay, you just make a living. Who are you?” she added.

“Just a guy and a piano,” he replied with a grin.

“I don’t think so,” she said, picking up a CD off a table with his picture on the front of it.

“Okay, I’m a composer . . . a piano composer,” he said.

It was obvious to Madi that he was someone very important, perhaps even popular, but their worlds were very opposite. *I’m boots and rodeos, and he’s Bach and Beethoven.*

“Would you like a popsicle?” he asked Ally. She quickly looked back at her mother who nodded yes.

“Would you like one too?” he asked Madi.

“No, thank you.”

“Look in the freezer and bring me a purple one,” he said.

Ally hopped up and coerced Lady to follow her to the kitchen just inside the door.

"Okay, you know what I do. What about you?" he asked.

"I am a professional barrel racer," she replied, not sure if he would know what that was.

"Really! Are you from a rodeo family?" he asked.

Shocked at his knowledge, she smiled and said, "I am. My dad roped professionally back in the day."

Not wanting to be too nosy and curious, he asked, "Ally's dad? Does he rodeo?"

"No, he was a football player and farmer. He passed away two years ago," she answered.

"I'm sorry to hear that, and I'm sorry for your loss," he replied, not knowing if he struck a nerve.

A purple popsicle appeared in his face. "Here you go," Ally said.

He chuckled. "Thank you."

"Mom," Ally started, lips red from her popsicle, "I want to learn to play the piano."

"Well, maybe we can look into that when we get home," she said.

"I'll make a deal with you. You keep that bird at bay and I'll teach you," Michael said.

Ally's eyes lit up over a big grin.

"We don't want to bother you with—"

"You're not, I would love to. Plus I give lessons at home."

"Well . . ."

"Oh Mom, please!" Ally begged.

"Monday, Wednesday, and Friday, one hour a day. How's that sound? We'll start next week," he said to both of them.

Madi shook her head with a grin. "Okay."

Chapter 11

A few days had passed since Michael had seen Madi and Ally. This morning he was in the middle of his grueling gym workout, out of breath, trying to suck down a bottle of water. *You're killing me!* He was only about twenty minutes into his session when he heard a door shut behind him.

"Look, Mom—it's Michael."

Before turning to see the girls, he took a deep breath and mustered up the strength to pretend he was in better shape. "Hey, guys," he said. Just saying two words about killed him.

"Hello," Madi said, trying not to show any expression of her thoughts. *A composer and gorgeous.*

Ally ran up to him and gave him a big hug; he grimaced at the pain as it radiated up his spin.

Madi giggled. *But not in shape.*

Michael made his way over to the wall and leaned against it before he fell out in front of them.

"Have you been working out long?" she asked.

"Oh, yeah, I work out a lot," he said, hoping she wouldn't see the truth. *Being a farm girl and a rodeo girl she's probably tough as nails*, he thought.

"You ready to get back to work?" a young lady asked as she walked from the back of the room.

"Sure," he replied, holding up one hand. She could tell he hadn't caught his breath.

Turning to Madi, the trainer asked, "Can I help you guys?"

"I'd like to join for a few months, if you do short-term," Madi said.

"Of course. My name is Deanne. Come over and we'll fill out some paperwork," she replied.

"Have fun!" Madi smiled at Michael as she walked past. It was obvious he wasn't fooling her; he was turning red, trying not to breathe too heavily.

The door closed again and he turned to see the athletic elderly couple entering the gym, headed straight for the treadmills. The man stopped and faced Michael. "Say, are you the young man staying at the Abbotts' cottage?"

"I am," Michael said.

The lady perked up. "Oh, I hope Lady isn't being any trouble," she said.

"Lady belongs to you?" he asked.

"Yes. The couple that used to own that cottage always fed her in the morning and she got used to going over to visit. We were happy to see someone buy it; Lady has seemed depressed until you showed up," she said.

Michael laughed. "She's welcome anytime."

"She likes the piano," Ally piped up.

"She does?" the lady asked. "Is she yours?" she asked, looking at Michael.

Michael was a little shocked at the question. "No, just a friend," he answered.

"Mom's in the back filling out paperwork," Ally replied, throwing her thumb over her shoulder and toward the office.

"We're the Hentises. Let us know if you need anything or if Lady is being a nuisance," the man said, speeding up his treadmill.

Madi walked out of the office and folded the paper into

her back pocket. She smiled at the couple she recognized from jogging.

"Hey, Mama, these are the people that Lady belongs to," Ally said.

"Hi, how are you?" Madi said politely to the couple.

They answered with a smile and wave, much like they did when running on the street.

Deanne came out of the back. "You ready to get back at it?" she asked Michael.

He was relieved to have had a few minutes of rest. "Sure." His answer wasn't convincing, but Deanne didn't care.

"Bye, Michael," Ally said.

"See you, kiddo," he replied to Ally.

Madi stopped in her tracks and stared at him with an expression he couldn't quite read. *What did I say?* Michael thought. Madi's expression broke into a smile—kiddo was a common nickname around the farm from her dad and Cole.

"Maybe we'll see you on the beach," Madi said to Michael.

"Most definitely." He smirked, still not sure what the funny look was for.

Walking out, she overheard the lady on the treadmill whisper to her husband, "Do you know who that is? That's Michael Curry!" *Hmm. He's got fans here. So how famous is he*? she thought.

ॐ

That evening Michael closed his eyes and ran his hands over the keys again, preparing himself to finish his new piece. The melodies had come so easily a week ago. Still, he couldn't focus and settle his mind. *Man, what's going on? I can't think. Was it that hard of a workout?* He took a deep breath and started over with his ritual, again with no concentration. Then it dawned on him: he couldn't stop thinking about her. *I don't need this right now. Plus, she's not interested in me.*

He heard Lady outside the door. Opening it, he bent down and said, “It’s kinda late for you to be out.” Without waiting for the invite, she waddled up the steps into the back porch. After walking in a few circles under the piano she settled into her normal spot. “Well, I’m glad you’re here. I need some help,” he said, sitting back down. Taking another deep breath he stretched out his hands and fingers and went into his new piece with his inspiration under the piano.

“Ahhh. There it is,” Madi said, listening to the tunes sweeping across the street and into her opened bedroom window. *I almost feel like he’s playing, well, talking to me. Such a nice guy and funny. Single. Successful. Sweet to people. Sweet to Ally. Very classy. Clean! Generous. Oh my gosh! Why am I thinking about him? He’s probably not interested in a girl like me.*

Madi rolled over and snuggled up to Ally. “Sweet pea, you will always be my number one,” she whispered while running her fingers through her sleeping child’s hair.

Chapter 12

A few days had passed; Ally had begun her piano lessons, but Michael hadn't had much time to visit with Madi. He was standing at the kitchen window when he heard the little voice outside: "Just knock on his door."

"Shhh. You don't have to holler it," Madi said to Ally as they cut through to the beach.

He threw the dishtowel in the sink and rushed to the back door. "Hey, strangers," he said, leaning out.

"I told you he was up," Ally said.

Madi turned red with embarrassment. Michael tried not to smile.

"You want to come outside with us?" Ally asked. Now Michael could really see the red coming through on Madi's cheeks.

"Have you got room?" he asked, trying to fish out Madi's thoughts.

"Of course, silly. It's a big beach." Ally giggled.

"I'll be right out," he said, closing the door.

Madi was setting out her plastic Adirondack chair and umbrella when she saw his screen door swing open and Lady climbing down the two steps. Michael walked out carrying his folding beach chair and a towel around his neck. He had changed into a pair of navy blue board shorts and a V-neck shirt that allowed the definition in his arms and chest to show. Apparently the gym time was paying off.

Madi stopped for a second and stared at him walking toward her. *Dang!*

"You ladies don't mind if I join you?" he said to break the ice.

"No, pull up some sand," Madi replied.

Setting his chair down, his aviators slid off his face and fell to the sand. Madi picked them up and handed them to him. "Thanks," he said with a big smile.

She held the glasses for a moment too long before he reached for them. *What the hell am I doing?* She blushed again.

"It feels good to just sit," he said, watching Ally play in the water.

"So you have been busy writing at night?" Madi asked.

"Is it too loud or late?" Michael said, shocked she could hear him.

"No, it's nice," she replied. A squeal caught their attention as Ally splashed in a wave. "How is writing going?" she asked.

"Good, I think. I feel like I've had writer's block for some time. And having deadlines doesn't help."

"Deadlines?"

"I have a new tour coming up and I am supposed to have new material to release. Even though I'll get something written here I still have studio time . . . just time-consuming." He felt as though he was starting to dump problems and changed the subject. "What about you?" he asked.

"Just here clearing my head and letting my horse heal from a crash we had," she said. She pulled her hat down to cover her eyes.

"Crash? Vehicle?" he asked, confused.

"No, we were at a rodeo and he took a bad step and fell coming out of the arena."

Michael looked over at her. "Is he or she going to be okay?"

"Yes, he will be fine. He just needs some rest." She smiled

at his concern. "Back to you. I heard the lady on the treadmill the other day recognize you."

He smiled. "Yeah, she asked a million questions."

"When is this next tour?"

"It starts in October," he said.

"Wow, that's coming up fast."

"Yeah, it's kind of a weird situation. My promoters want to release a surprise album during the tour. Not the norm for tours."

"Michael, come get in." Ally had come and grabbed hold of his right arm.

"Ally, he probably doesn't want to right now."

"No, it's okay. It's a shame I haven't been in yet," he said. He stood up and took off his Ray-Bans and placed them in the chair. Kicking off his flip-flops he peeled off his shirt and threw it on top of his glasses. Madi's eyes widened at his toned chest and arms. *For someone who hasn't worked out long, he looks good.* She was relying on her sunglasses to hide the expression, and watched as her new neighbor and friend played in the water with her daughter.

After a few minutes she heard her invite. "Come on, Mommy!" Ally yelled. Madi wasn't going to miss the invitation from the little brown-haired girl who owned her heart.

"Oh my gosh, it's cold!" she said in a high-pitched voice.

"You'll get used to it. Come in," Ally coached her.

"This is far enough for me," she said.

"It's not too bad once you get in," Michael encouraged her. She stepped back onto the sand and placed her Fedora hat and glasses down. Then, turning, she took a running start and dove in. Coming to the top of the water she heard Michael: "That's impressive!"

She grabbed Ally and swung her around in the water; Ally squealed with excitement. Michael watched the mother and daughter wrestle and splash each other. *A perfect picture*, he thought. But that changed when they nodded to each other and turned, maliciously wading toward him. "You two aren't tough enough," he said before they leaped, shrieking with laughter and pushing his head under.

"Now I'm cold," Madi said after several minutes of play fighting, as she walked out of the water and onto the beach. She covered her chest with her folded arms and shivered in place while waiting for Ally to exit. Madi turned to run to her chair but found Michael standing in front of her holding her towel open. "Thank you," she said. But what was sweeter to her was when he opened Ally's towel and gave her the same treatment. He was such a gentleman and Madi appreciated his willingness to be defeated in the great water battle by her and her little fireball.

Lady was patiently waiting for them under Michael's chair. "Can I get her some water?" Ally asked.

"That would be a good idea. She has a bowl on the back porch," Michael said.

"She has a bowl now?" Madi said, smiling.

He just smirked. They positioned their chairs to watch Ally and Lady run to the cottage. Madi placed her towel on her chair underneath her since her teal two-piece bathing suit had nearly dried.

"So tell me about home," Michael asked.

"Well, there's not much to tell. We live on my parents' farm and I travel a lot with rodeos. Ally is homeschooled. I don't know, what do you want to know?" she replied.

"Tell me about the farm," he said.

"It's beautiful. I guess I'm prejudiced because I grew up there. But we grow hay and during this time of year the fields are a greenish, bluish color. When the wind blows it looks like water; you can see the wind before it gets to you." Michael smiled at the vision she painted.

"All my life I would lie in the field and imagine I was traveling all over the world. It sounds crazy but the fields almost have a magic sense to them; you have to experience it to understand," she said.

"Sounds incredible," he replied.

"It is. It's imaginational magic," she added.

Wow! What a beautiful term, imaginational magic, he thought.

"Tell me about Ally's dad." Michael didn't want to push anything but felt like it was the right question.

"Cole. He was a great father and husband. We were high school sweethearts, first love. He was a great football player and should have gone pro but got injured. He was a good farmer, like my dad."

"I'm sorry for your loss," he said.

"I miss him," she said softly. "Ally misses him."

"Does she like to fish?" he said, feeling like it was time to change the subject.

"Yes! Dad has been the only one to take her since Cole died."

"Would you care if I took you guys?" Michael asked.

"I think she would like that."

"What about you?"

Madi glanced over at him. "I would too."

Chapter 13

Madi sat on her front porch enjoying coffee that Michael had given her. The sun peeked out from beyond the palm trees on the far end of the street. She believed she had a front-row seat to both sunrise and sunset. Everything was quiet on the street with only the seagulls crying out as they dipped beyond Michael's rooftop.

His front door swung open and he and Lady strolled across the street to Madi's cottage.

"Are you sure she's not yours?" Madi said with a grin.

"I am starting to wonder that myself. How are you this morning?"

"I'm good and this coffee is good," she said.

"What do you girls have planned for today?" Michael asked.

"Not much. I'm sure we'll go to the beach."

"How about that fishing trip?" he asked.

Madi nodded her head. "We'd like that."

"Good. I'll be by in thirty minutes."

Madi swallowed. "Thirty minutes? You don't give a girl much time to get ready," she said.

"Ready? We're going fishing. Do you need more time?" he asked with a laugh.

"No, we'll manage," she said, smiling.

Walking back to his cottage he could feel Madi watching him

from the doorway. She loved his casual dress—cargo shorts, a button-down shirt over a T-shirt, and flip-flops. *He is so laid-back about everything.*

Ally perked up from the breakfast table. “Was that a horn?”

Madi walked to the front window and saw Michael walking up from his golf cart. “Are you ready?” Michael said. Madi turned to Ally.

A knock sounded from the front screen door. “Come on in—we’re almost ready,” Madi said.

Ally greeted Michael in the foyer with a question. “What kind of fishing are we doing?”

“Well, I don’t know. Salt-water fishing, I guess.”

“Ally, come get your bag,” Madi hollered from the kitchen.

Michael walked in to find Madi stressed about gathering their things. “Can I help?”

Without an answer she pushed a beach bag into his arms and threw two towels on top, taking two steps toward the living room. “I’m sorry, I don’t know what I’m thinking.” She tried to take the bag back.

“It’s okay, I don’t mind. We’re just going fishing,” he said, amused by the mayhem.

She smiled. *Girls don’t “just go fish.” He’ll figure it out soon enough. Crap! What am I thinking? We’re not dating. Madi, stay focused.*

After locking the front door Madi saw that the backseat of the cart was taken up by a large ice chest.

“Here, I’ll take that,” he said, taking the rest of her things and resting them on top of the cooler.

“I love golf carts,” Ally said, jumping in the front seat.

“Have you ever driven one?” he asked.

“No, she hasn’t, and I don’t think she’s ready,” Madi said, worried that Ally would wreck them.

“Oh, I bet she is.” He slid in front of the wheel and motioned for Ally to sit in his lap. “You steer and I’ll work the brake and gas." Ally's smile was bigger than her face; it wasn't something Madi could argue about.

The cart sped off down the street, weaving back and forth across the lane. Ally laughed loudly while Madi hung on and coached her, "Left . . . no right . . . left . . . " Michael smiled but laughed inside at Madi's reaction. It was clear to him that she couldn't relax; but his laugh turned serious when he thought she probably hadn't relaxed since Cole's death.

They met the Hentises coming around the corner—Mr. Hentise jolted to the left and Mrs. Hentise ducked to the right.

"Sorry! Lady's back at the house. We're going fishing!" Michael yelled as they sped past.

"Oh my gosh, we almost hit them!" Madi said as her hair flipped in the wind.

"I saw them," Ally assured her.

"Turn here." Michael pointed to the right. The one-way road led them in front of a few restaurants, the public pier, and Randy's Bar and Grill.

"Didn't we just pass it?" Madi asked.

"We not fishing on the pier," Michael said, pointing. "Turn here and stop in front of that sign." He slammed on the brakes a little too roughly, causing their bodies to shift forward and the cart to come to a sliding stop.

"Wheeeee!" Ally yelled.

"We're taking a charter boat?" Madi asked.

"Yeah." Michael seemed confused at her surprise.

They stepped out of the cart to find a young kid taking their cooler. "Hello, Mr. Curry. I'm Jake the deckhand. Y'all climb on aboard and I'll get the rest of your things."

Madi grabbed her bag. "I didn't know you were chartering a boat."

"I thought it would be fun to get out on the gulf. What do you think?" he asked Ally. But she was too busy taking the deckhand's directions and wasted no time jumping down into the boat. White smoke shot out from behind the forty-two-foot Hatteras as the captain fired up the twin diesel engines.

"Good morning, Mr. Curry. You've picked a great day to fish. You must be Ms. Madi and Miss Ally," a gray-headed man said as he climbed down from the bridge.

"Hi." Ally stuck her hand out.

The old man smiled. "You want to be second mate today?"

"Sure. Do I get to drive?"

"We'll see," he said, laughing and untying the boat as the young deckhand quickly boarded.

"I feel like this is too much," Madi whispered, feeling guilty.

"Nonsense, let's have some fun." Michael opened the cooler and handed her a bottle of water.

Jake pulled out four rod-and-reels and began rigging them for a day at sea. The curiosity quickly overwhelmed Ally and she was promptly in the middle of Jake's business.

"Let me know if she's in the way," Madi told Jake.

"No, ma'am, she's fine."

The captain had barely cleared the jetties before slamming the throttle forward and winding the engines out at full speed ahead.

They were ten minutes into the trip when Ally came to Madi. "Mama, I don't feel good." She was white as a ghost and holding her stomach.

"Oh, no, I think she's seasick," Madi said.

"If we need to go back in we can," Michael assured Madi.

Jake leaned into the conversation. "Hey, Ally, keep your eyes on those buildings." He pointed toward shore. "Once we start fishing, she'll be okay."

Five minutes later he had a line in the water and immediately hollered, "Fish on!" In a flash, Ally's color came back and she was on Jake's heels waiting for the rod.

Chapter 14

After a great morning of fishing the captain tied the boat to the pier of an uninhibited island, and Jake exited the cabin with a backpack and giant basket filled with breads and other sides.

"We're eating lunch here?" Madi asked.

"Yep, it was part of the fishing package. I have no clue what to expect," Michael whispered to her.

"Expect good fish and drinks," the captain replied.

"Your hearing is exceptional," Michael said, embarrassed that he had been overheard.

"I don't know why, since I've been running these loud boats all my life. You folks go ahead. I'll get the drinks."

"We don't mind helping," Madi said, reaching for the cooler. Michael beat her to it and started down the dock.

The island was small with only a few palms and underbrush, and the beaches were snow-white and fine like sugar. Madi had been so focused on slopping sunscreen on Ally all morning that she had forgotten to use it herself. Michael noticed her pressing her skin to see how red she was getting.

"Do you want me to help you with that lotion?" he asked.

"Thanks." She handed him the bottle and pulled back her hair.

"It'll be twenty or thirty minutes before lunch is ready if you folks want to swim or cruise the island," the captain said while cleaning the fish they had caught that morning.

"You want to go walk?" Michael asked.

"Sure. Do you want to come?" she asked Ally, who watched the captain clean the fish.

"I'll catch up. I want to watch," she replied, never looking up.

As Madi and Michael walked along the beach, she turned to him and said, "Thank you for this. I didn't expect this kind of treatment."

"I thought it would be fun. I have a surprise for Ally once we get back on the boat."

"What's that?" she curiously asked.

Michael saw her eyes widen. "I'll leave it for a surprise to you too."

"Gee thanks." She pushed him. "Okay, question time. You ask, we both answer, then my turn. Okay?" Madi said. They walked slowly, almost staggering in their steps.

"Okay. Shoot!" Michael said.

"Favorite food?" she asked.

Michael thought for a moment. "I like almost anything, but I'd say seafood."

"Okay, steak for me," she answered.

"Favorite drink?" he asked.

Madi quickly answered, "Beer!" She started laughing. "I answered that too fast. You're going to think I'm a lush."

Laughing with her, Michael answered his own question. "Wine for me."

Madi put her hand to her chin. "Umm . . . favorite place?"

"It's starting to be here," he said.

"Not here," she added.

"Okay. Then I would say . . . Africa."

"Really?"

"Yes, I have a close friend there. And I've toured there many times and done some mission work," he answered.

Mission work! Wow, that's impressive. I would love to do that.

Suddenly a fish head with the guts stringing out of the gills appeared in Michael's face. "Pretty gross, huh!?" Ally said, holding it with a long stick.

"Ally!" Madi snapped.

"It's okay," he laughed.

Ally ran off to toss the head into the water.

"She's such a tomboy," Madi replied.

"Were you a tomboy?" he asked.

"Are you kidding? I beat up all the boys until I was a junior in high school."

They sat down and watched Ally play in the water while they talked about their pasts and quirks. Madi was surprised to hear that he'd grown up in an orphanage as she learned the story of Robin and Doug taking him in.

After his story, she couldn't hold back any longer with a question that had been burning for a while. "No girlfriends? Wives?"

"I've dated a few girls, but they always turned out to be friends. Being on tour for so long, I just never had time to settle down," he smoothly answered.

"Do you regret that?" *Why did I ask that?* she thought after saying it.

"No and yes. I'm happy but I know I'm not one to be alone. I was alone for so many years, and when Robin and Doug came along, I felt like I belonged for the first time."

Madi looked up at the puffy clouds hanging above them. "I love lying in the field and watching those types of clouds."

Michael glanced up. "I would always make animals out of the shapes."

She smiled and gazed at him. "Me too."

While they watched imaginative animals swirl above them, a loud raspy voice shouted out, "Dinner time!" They stood to their feet, and Madi coached Ally to follow them back to the makeshift fire in a pile of rocks and a blanket spread out on the sand.

"Wow, it smells amazing!" Madi said.

"When you do this for thirty years you get pretty good at it. Do you folks mind if I say grace?"

Madi looked at Michael to see his reaction; he nodded for the captain to continue. "God, help us take care of the ocean. Be with the boat and crew. Be with these fine folks and may their relationship be strong and adventurous. Bless these fish and the meal to keep us strong. Amen."

It was obvious that the captain wasn't sure of their relationship, and Michael giggled under his breath at Madi's blushing. *She sure gets embarrassed easy.*

The captain fixed a big plate and handed it to Ally. She held it frozen in motion, looking at all the food, then looked up at her mother.

"Just eat what you can," Madi mouthed to her.

He then fixed a plate for Madi, then Michael, then his deckhand.

"This is incredible!" Madi said.

Jake saw Ally pushing her food around her plate. "Miss Ally, that's the fish you caught."

She smiled and entertained Jake by taking a bite, then her eyes lit up and she nodded her head. "I like this!" The pressure was off Madi.

"You folks enjoy. I got to go get the shark fishing tackle out and rig the poles," the captain said.

Ally's eyes got wide. "Shark fishing!"

Madi smiled and looked over at Michael. "That's a pretty good surprise."

Ally scarfed her plate down. "Can I go help the captain?"

"I don't know," Madi started to say.

"Don't worry, she can help me," Jake said, taking her plate. "Come on and I'll show you the hooks we use." He walked toward the dock with Ally prancing around him.

"So do you do this often?" Madi asked Michael.

"Oh yeah, you know, every weekend." He laughed.

Chapter 15

Madi heard the engines power down before she felt them. It appeared they were in the middle of nowhere when she looked up. She had fallen asleep after the immense meal on the beach and the sound of the twin diesels motoring them toward open water. She looked toward the front and found Ally and Michael standing on the bow; he was pointing to something in the water that had Ally's smile out in full force. Standing and waiting to catch her sea legs, she climbed on the walkway and headed to join them on the bow.

Upon reaching them she began to say something, but the forty-two-foot Hatteras suddenly sank between swells and threw her off balance. She fell forward onto Michael.

"Still sleepy?" he asked.

"I guess so," she said. *Oh my gosh, can I embarrass myself anymore today?* she thought.

"What are y'all looking at?" she asked.

"Dolphins! They're riding the bow!" Ally said in excitement.

She leaned over Ally's shoulder and peered down into the tranquil blue water just in time to see a dolphin's fin break the water. "Wow, that's awesome," shc said.

"They've been with us since we left the island," Ally replied.

The voice of the captain broke their concentration on the dolphins. "You guys ready to shark fish?"

Ally's eyes lit up. "What about the dolphins? The sharks will get them."

"No need to worry about them; sharks are scared of them. We are going to troll for a moment to let the dolphins head somewhere else," he said, holding an unlit cigar in his mouth. Michael laughed to himself thinking of Captain Quint in *Jaws*.

"I would normally not ask an eight-year-old, but after seeing you run around with a fish head and guts, I think it's safe. Do you want to help me chum?" Jake asked Ally.

Without answering she ran to the back of the boat behind him.

"Goodness, I didn't realize I was that tired. How long was I out?" Madi asked Michael.

"Maybe an hour."

"Holy cow, I'm sorry. Not very good company, and I didn't mean for you to watch Ally," she replied.

"Nonsense. We had fun. You looked peaceful." He smiled.

"You folks want to come hear this?" the captain asked. Joining the rest of the crew they listened to him give instructions on how to chum and what poles to use. He showed them a harness belt for the rod-and-reels to rest in. Madi was sure that she didn't want to strap herself into a rod that had a man-eating predator on the other end. Ally had fish guts and pig blood up to her forearms. "This is awesome!" she said. Madi made a disgusted face at the mess and smell that encompassed her.

Jake threw a couple of lines out in the water and set the rods in their appropriate holders. Then he pulled out a water line and hosed himself and Ally off.

They were barely set before one of the rods bowed over and the reel sang with the line spilling out. "Fish on!" the captain yelled.

Jake scrambled to the rod and took it out of the holder, looking toward Michael. "You want this one?"

"Let's see what the second mate has," he said, looking at Ally.

Jake motioned for her to sit in the chair that faced the rear of the boat; he placed the rod in a holder in front of her and held on to the pole. She struggled cranking the reel before the captain came down and adjusted the reel so she could handle it. The line quickly ran to the left side of the boat, and the captain scrambled to the bridge and swung the boat around, keeping the line off the rear.

Madi was smiling at her daughter fighting the rod-and-reel when another rod sang out and bent over. Madi screamed and jumped to the side.

"Fish on! And it's a big one!" the captain yelled. Michael saw the look in the young deckhand's eyes—he couldn't leave his post with Ally, but the other rod was now bent over.

"I got it," Michael told him. Michael motioned to Madi.

"I ride horses; I'm no shark wrangler," she said.

"Think of it like roping a calf," the captain said. His accent seemed to have morphed into British English. "Sheriff Broody, can you handle it?" The captain laughed. Michael laughed with him but Madi wasn't finding *Jaws* humor funny.

Michael handed her the belt with the rod holder attached. She looked at him like he was crazy. "Hell no!" she exclaimed.

He started laughing. "I'll help you."

"No and I mean no!" She stood her ground.

The line was steadily feeding out of the reel; Michael could only envision the line on the reel starting to smoke, he wondered if that was only in the movies.

"Ms. Madi, the Sheriff is gonna need some assistance," the captain said in his fake accent.

Just then, the rod shot forward and pulled Michael to the side of the boat. "Holy crap!" he shouted.

Now Madi was feeling like she was letting him down, so she inched forward to help. Jake and Ally were still fighting their shark; the boat was filled with excitement.

"Put the belt around me!" Michael shouted.

She grabbed the belt and swung to put it around him, only

to find herself knocking over the bucket of blood into the floor of the boat. She visualized the tin pail bouncing off the fiberglass floor on the boat and spilling the bloody chum in slow motion. Looking up at the captain standing above them on the bridge, she could see his mouth wide-open, holding his unlit cigar, and making a high-pitched squeaky noise.

"Sorry." She smiled. But he could only look on at his pride and joy that now looked like a scene from a horror show—with blood on his fiberglass floor and a screaming little girl who was landing her first shark.

She finally wrapped the belt around Michael, but before she could buckle it, she felt the boat take a dip between swells and fell to her hands and knees on the blood-soaked floor. The captain never lost his horrified expression as the tools of his trade became bloody horror flick movie props.

"Sorry." She smiled at him once again.

"What are you doing?" Michael asked, holding on to the rod with his life. Not knowing what to do, she regained her footing and wrapped the blood-soaked belt around his waist, finally buckling it.

Looking down at his now blood-spattered Italian silk shirt, he yelped, "What the hell?"

"Sorry," she said in the same soft embarrassed voice.

At that moment the back of the boat took another dip so hard it felt as if it was sinking. Madi screamed as she lost her footing again and grabbed Michael's shirt, pulling him back two steps. She almost had her feet underneath her when Michael's right foot shot up from losing traction against the fiberglass floor. For a short moment she felt as if they were dancing on a frozen pond.

To the poor captain, it all happened in slow motion. There was nothing he could do but watch.

Madi and Michael both came crashing down to the floor into the quarter inch of blood that waited for them. Michael hit first. Madi landed on top of him and quickly pulled up her legs and arms to avoid the maroon pond beneath them.

The rod shot out of Michael's hand, and between the slick floor and Madi balancing on top of him, he fought to grab the live rod dancing in the floor of the boat.

Madi reached for it and gripped the handle only for a second before the boat rocked back, causing her to lose grip. Both Michael and Madi watched as the rod ran up the side of the boat and over into the ocean.

They looked at each other, wide-eyed, then looked back up at the captain just in time to see his unlit cigar fall from his open mouth.

"My rod!"

Chapter 16

Robin looked down at her cell phone at the 407 area code. *That's a Florida area code,* she thought. She picked it up after the third ring. "Hello? Yes, this is Michael's manager." Doug looked up from his book; he could tell by Robin's expression she was anxious to get off the phone.

"Yes, I will let you know something today. He is only a couple of hours from there, so I am sure it will work out," she replied to the caller on the other end of the line. She looked back at Doug and grinned. "Thank you, you too." And she hung up.

"What was that about?" Doug asked, beating her to the question.

"That was the president of American Orphanages. They want to book Michael for a show at an amusement park in two weeks."

"He is supposed to be resting and writing. Those were your orders," Doug replied.

"Yes, I know, but you know how much he loves doing shows for orphanages," she said. Robin wasn't going to let Doug have any influence on the possible show or Michael's career—not that he ever did.

Knowing there was no use in trying to push the issue, Doug picked his book back up and returned to reading. He heard Robin leave Michael a message on his phone.

"So, do you want to go?" she asked Doug.

Looking over his reading glasses, he said, "You know how I feel about crowds."

"Well, I'm going, and I know Michael would like to see you," she said, avoiding eye contact.

Looking back at his book and reestablishing his place, he said, "I'll go."

With those words she jumped up and ran to her room like a teenager going on her first date. "Packing a little early, aren't we?" he shouted toward the stairs.

Michael, dripping sweat from his run, reached in his refrigerator for bottled water. Taking a gulp, he saw his phone light up with a missed call from Robin. He walked into the bathroom, grabbed a towel, wiped his face and hands, then hit redial on his phone. "Hey, sorry I missed your call. What's up?" he asked Robin.

After she explained everything, he said, "I'll do it, but let me get back with you. I might need two rooms."

There was a pause on the phone. "Two?" she asked.

"I'll fill you in later, but I might bring a friend and her daughter."

"What's this *later* business? Who is she?" Robin quickly interjected.

Michael always thought she was nosy when it came to his love life, or what little of his personal life existed. "It's nothing special. She's just a friend who is staying across the street." He wasn't interested in explaining everything at that moment. Mostly because he really wasn't sure where he stood with Madi.

"Okay, I'll send you all the information and call you the day before," she said.

"Cool."

"How's writing?" she asked.

"Really good. I am having all kinds of thoughts and putting some things on paper. I'm glad I came here to clear my head," he said.

"Good! Let me know if there is anything you need."

"Okay, talk to you later." And he hung up the phone.

Not wanting to ask at the last moment, Michael walked over to Madi's. Lady met him halfway there. "You know you're not going to be able to come in Madi's house," he said. Lady just looked up at him with her tongue hanging out and teeth showing, as if she understood everything he said.

Ally answered the door. "Lady!" she yelled, bending down and hugging her.

Lady looked back at Michael as if to say, "Don't worry, I'm not going in."

Madi walked around the corner with a dishtowel in hand. "Hey, I see you brought your sidekick," she said.

"Yeah, she joined me on the street," Michael answered.

"I was talking to Lady," she smiled at him.

"Oh, haha." He smirked. She possessed the sense of humor he liked, and her quirkiness was attractive.

"I'm teasing you. Come in," she said.

"Ally, why don't you go and play with Lady? She looks like she could use the exercise," she added. Ally slapped her side and told Lady to come, like she was a working a cow dog.

"Can I get you something to drink?" Madi asked, since it looked like he'd been running.

"No, I'm good. Thank you," he said.

She went back to the kitchen and finished drying the dishes. Not giving him a chance to explain his visit, she thanked him and talked about their fishing trip.

Michael watched as she dried the dishes and talked; she was wearing workout shorts and a tight-fitting white shirt that showed her petite figure. She definitely didn't have the legs of a barrel racer, or at least how he had imagined barrel racers' legs to look—namely having scars from hitting barrels at high speeds. Her legs were tan and carried a reflection that showed the smoothness and softness of each curve. Her hair was down and it bounced as she worked at drying a cutting board. Part of her shirt was wet from the soapy water, and either she didn't care if he saw, or she was oblivious to it.

"Well?" she asked. Michael, having not listened to anything she had said, scrambled for words. She smiled at the notion that he was looking at her and not listening to her.

"What?" he softly asked.

"Is the captain ever going to let us fish with him again?" she asked, giggling.

"Oh! Yeah! He's fine. I paid for the rod even though he insisted that you pay him."

"What! He said that?" she said, shocked. Michael smiled and there was a short moment of pause. "Oh, you jackass," she said and threw the towel at him.

"Okay, the reason I came over is that I have a concert at an amusement park, just north of here, in two weeks and wanted to know if you and Ally would like to join me," he said.

She looked up with an expression that caught him off guard. Was it one of shock or confusion?

"I will book two rooms, one for me and the other for you two," he quickly added, hoping that would ease the funny look.

But she didn't say anything, causing Michael to second-guess his invitation.

Madi turned back to the sink. "I don't know," she said.

"Okay, well you don't have to. I just wanted to ask," he said softly.

She looked down at her shirt. "I'll be right back." And she stormed to her room with her head down.

Man, what did I say? Maybe I should have said something about her shirt. Thoughts raced through his head about her quick exit. After a few minutes of waiting, it was obvious she wasn't returning anytime soon. He walked toward the door and paused for a moment to see if he could hear her coming out—nothing. He left and walked across the front yard, but before he reached the street, he stopped and turned around. *No, I'm not giving up!*

He walked back into the cottage and up to her bedroom door. He started to knock on the door when he heard her sobbing inside. Pushing the door open he found her lying on her bed with her head buried in her pillow. He gently sat down beside her and put his hand on her back, massaging and rubbing in a circular motion. "Hey, I'm sorry if I said something," he quietly said, thinking that something about the amusement park must have sparked a memory.

She sat up, still sobbing. "I'm sorry, this isn't fair to you," she said.

"I don't want to do or say anything to make you upset," he said, realizing something had provoked a memory of her late husband.

"It's okay," she said, sniffling, realizing her shirt was wet.

She got up and scrambled through her clothes looking for a dry shirt. Michael stood up and made his way to the doorway. "Are you going to be okay?" he asked.

"Yeah," she said, looking down at the shirt she had picked out.

With that, Michael slipped out the front door, still uncertain of her feelings and of what he'd said to make her cry.

Chapter 17

Later that night, Madi ventured out onto her front porch alone as she sipped on her cabernet sauvignon. There was a warm breeze in the night air and she could feel the salty moisture on her skin. She rocked back and forth on the rocking chair, her legs pulled up and her feet planted under her. Between the warm breezes, she could hear the soft notes floating across the street from Michael's porch. Thinking about her actions earlier in the day, she wondered if she had scared him off. She hoped that wasn't the case.

Madi closed her eyes and pictured the last family vacation she and Cole had planned. Two months before the freak accident, they had decided to go to the same amusement park. Five days before they left, the accident occurred. Madi remembered staring at the tickets in the hospital, knowing Cole was hurrying to cut the hay so that they could make their trip. She couldn't help but feel the tickets played a major part of taking his life as well as halting hers.

A strong wind pushed through the porch, and she opened her eyes long enough to wipe her tears. She set down the half-empty glass, closed her eyes again, and rocked slowly. She visualized herself back in the fields of Alicia, listening to the laughter of her little girl on the tire swing. Then she saw a figure in the field, the grass chest-high on the image of a man walking toward her. A warm gentle smile welcomed her—it was Cole's. The top two buttons were undone on his denim shirt, and his dark-colored hair was pushed to the side. It was his familiar appearance before he sank into the coma, losing his weight and muscular form.

She had imagined him many times since his death, but this time was different—it was closer to a dream and had a magical flare.

"Hey, angel." His voice was followed by a slight echo. He reached for her hand and for the first time, she could feel the warmth of his body.

"Is this real?" she asked.

"Somewhat," he replied.

"I miss you!" She began to cry.

"I like him, Madi," he said.

She knew he was speaking about Michael. "I would never do that to you," she said. Then he gripped her hand and she could feel his strength, something she had never experienced in her imagination.

"To me?" he questioned. "It's not about me. It's about you and Ally," he added. She lowered her head at his words. "Madi, I can give a lot, but the greatest is . . ."

A strong wind blew across her face, waking her from her imagination.

She opened her eyes wide and looked around; she couldn't make out if that had been a dream or just her thoughts. *I felt him, I heard him. It couldn't have been a dream.* Standing she reached for her wineglass to find it empty. *Okay, that's strange. Did I imagine drinking the wine too?*

The music from across the street stopped. She stood, paused at the screen door for a moment, then proceeded to the kitchen to refill her glass.

Returning to the front porch she saw someone approaching from the street—someone wearing a long-sleeved button-down shirt. Coming into the glow of light from the kitchen, she could see the top two buttons undone on Michael's shirt. The sight of his similarity to Cole sent chills up her spine.

"I hope you don't mind me walking over; I saw your light on," he said.

"No, I don't mind." Her voice was reassuring to him. "Would you like a glass?" she asked.

"Sure," he replied. He sat in the rocking chair on the other side of the front door.

"Tonight felt like a wine night. I hope you like it," she said, handing him the glass of red.

"I'm sure I will. I enjoy reds," he replied. Sitting back in her chair, she was still a little disturbed with her vision and the coincidence of Michael's choice of clothing.

"I'm sorry about my reaction today," she started.

"It's okay. I just wanted to come apologize for bringing up memories." He took a sip of the wine.

"It's fine. Really. I was surprised it did. The last vacation we had planned with Cole was at that same amusement park," she said. "But, Ally and I would love to go."

Her answer surprised him. "Are you sure?" he asked.

"Yes, I am sure. Ally wanted to go last time and I would love to see her face at the sight of the roller coasters. What do I need to pay?"

"Nothing," he answered a little defensively. "I don't expect you to pay. We just met."

At her look, he thought for a moment. "You can pay for supper one night. But really, everything is paid for."

"Well, it will be fun. Where is your concert?" she asked.

"Center stage," he replied not thinking anything of it.

"Oh, just center stage." She smirked.

He could hear Gus's feathers ruffling inside the screen door. "How's the attack bird?"

"Preparing for his next fight," she said, laughing.

Another strong breeze came through the front porch, and a familiar odor reached Michael's nostrils.

Madi noticed him smelling the air. “Is that what I think it is?” she asked.

“Yep, I believe so.”

“There’s nobody but old folks around here. I’m glad Ally is asleep,” she said.

“I don’t think there is an age limit to burn one,” he said, and they both laughed at the thought of two elderly people smoking pot.

They spent the rest of the night talking and laughing at each other’s stories of growing up and of places they had traveled. A few hours after midnight, full of good stories, a growing friendship, and wine, they finished off the bottle of red.

Chapter 18

The sun surged past the horizon and brought a new day to the small Florida island. Michael sat in one of the plastic Adirondack chairs watching the sunrise. He hadn't slept but a few hours during the night, thinking instead about his upcoming concert, but mostly thinking about Madi. He had never planned to meet someone during his rest period but she was bringing much inspiration to his writing, as well as some feelings he hadn't had in over a year—since Tessa.

He heard moaning coming from farther down the beach. Walking out onto the sand to investigate, he found a couple just a few hundred feet down the beach. He wasn't interested in interfering with their business but the man was rubbing his head and looked disoriented. Walking up to the man, Michael asked, "Are you okay?"

The man squinted his eyes at Michael; the sunlight was blinding, and his head full of matted gray hair draped over his hand as he held it over his eyes. "I could use some water," the old man said. Michael quickly jogged back to his cottage for a glass of water.

Upon returning he found the lady was now awake; he handed the glass to the man.

"Thanks, bro," the old man said.

Bro?

After the lady took a sip she said, "Thank you, young man."

Michael noticed the pipe that was stashed in the mangled sleeping bag they shared. *That explains the smell last night. Wait till Madi hears about this.*

"Do you guys live around here?" Michael asked.

"Yeah. My man, that chateau there is our humble estate," the man said, pointing to the blue cottage on stilts. He reached down and fumbled for his small, round, blue-tinted sunglasses, giving Michael flashbacks of old John Lennon pictures.

It became apparent that this couple never left the '60s. Reaching his hand out, he said, "I'm Michael."

"Hello, Michael, I'm Webster, and this is my loving bride, Sunshine," he said.

You just can't make up a story like this, Michael thought.

"I just love hearing you play," Sunshine complimented him.

"Right on, man! You can throw down on those keys. We should play someday," Webster said.

"Yeah, that would be fun," Michael said.

"Well, I don't want to bother you folks anymore. If you need anything just let me know," Michael said, picking up his glass.

"Hey, we are having a seafood broil tonight. Why don't you bring that sweet little lady and you guys come hang out with the locals?" Webster said.

"That sounds like fun but she has a little girl, and I wouldn't want to bring her to a grown-up party."

"No man, everyone on the street will be there. Totally safe. No partying," the man said, tucking his pipe away.

"Okay, sounds like fun. What can I bring?"

"Nothing, we'll divvy up after we buy everything."

"Sounds good, see you there." And Michael walked back to his cottage.

Looking back he saw the couple snuggled up next to each other. The old man's arm was around the lady while they watched the sunrise. *Now that's cool.*

Walking onto his back porch, an idea hit him and he

immediately sat down at the piano. Foregoing his normal ritual, he began to play a few chords. He took out his pad and jotted down the notes on the paper. *Why not? I don't see why it wouldn't work–though nobody else is doing this.* He played back through the chords that led to a chorus, and before he realized, he was adding more. He was elated with the inspiration that came to him despite the amount of sleep he had gotten the night before.

⁂

It was midmorning before Madi opened her eyes to a little girl with a parrot perched on her shoulder. "You look like a pirate," she said, yawning.

"That's what we have been playing!" Ally said.

"I'll fix breakfast." Madi rolled out of bed and grabbed her robe.

Pouring milk into the bowl of cereal, Madi said, "I have some exciting news."

"What's that?" Ally answered.

She bent down to Ally's level and peered into her beautiful eyes. "We are going to an amusement park next week!"

Ally's eyes widened. "Are we really?"

"Yep, Michael has a concert and has asked us to go." Madi turned to place the box of cereal back in the cabinet as Ally shoveled a spoon into her mouth.

"Are you and Michael boyfriend-girlfriend?" she asked, munching with her mouth open.

Madi turned and just stared. Pausing for a moment, she answered, "No, we are just friends."

"Oh, okay. I like him and it would be okay if y'all were."

Madi smiled as she turned back to the sink. She knew her daughter's innocence was showing, but she also knew the wisdom a child could have toward life.

Chapter 19

Ally ran to reach the beach; Madi walked behind her. Once past Michael's cottage the sea breeze hit them. The roar of the breaking waves muffled the seagulls flying above them, searching the salt water washing up on the sand. The waves seemed murderous and the height of them pounded hard against the water, causing the sea foam to increase. Ally froze halfway to their spot, examining the large waves and the violence wreaking havoc on their once-quiet beach.

Madi stood beside her. "The waves are really big today," she said. She could see the fear in Ally's eyes and was relieved that it scared her—she wouldn't need to lecture her about the waves today.

Madi found only one of her chairs. Looking around for the other, she saw it closer to Michael's cottage where he had left it early that morning. As she walked to retrieve it Michael walked out of his cottage. "Hey, sorry. I'll take it back down there," he said.

Madi smiled at his attire—plaid shorts, white tank with an unbuttoned Hawaiian shirt, and boat shoes—all classy, all the time. "Did you get any sleep?" she asked.

"No. You?" he asked.

"No," she said, smiling. She hadn't stayed up all night talking in a long time, and it felt good. But right now she felt like she was going to pass out from exhaustion.

"You know the ocean is pretty rough today. Is Ally wanting to swim?" he asked.

"Yes, but I won't let her in with it this rough." Ally was still sitting in the chair waiting for her mother to return. "Maybe we'll try it later," Madi said, looking out into the distance at a storm approaching.

Before she could yell at Ally, she was making her way toward them with a slight frown.

"Well, this was a short trip to the beach." Madi smiled at Michael.

"Mom, can we watch that movie now?" Ally asked. It was apparent that Madi had coached her to be outside versus watching a movie.

"Yes," she said.

"Would you like to see a princess movie?" Ally asked Michael.

Michael looked at Madi for approval. "Only if you want to," Madi said.

Michael looked back down at Ally who was wearing a large straw hat and sunglasses that were too big for her face. "I believe I would."

After retrieving the other chair from the beach and stashing it outside Michael's door, they walked across the street. Ally opened the front door and Michael followed the pair.

It looked like slow motion to Michael—Ally sidestepped to her right, Madi ducked, then a flurry of green feathers was in his face. He raised his forearms for protection and swatted up toward the ceiling, flailing his arms around and screaming like a little girl.

After Gus felt like Michael had enough, he glided back to his perch on top of his cage. The attack lasted only a few seconds, but the damage to Michael's ego was done.

Michael stood in the hall with two or three feathers stuck

in his messy hair. The girls were shocked. Then Madi couldn't hold it in any longer—a giggle broke out into a hysterical laugh.

"That's the devil's bird," Michael said, not amused.

"Oh my gosh, I'm sorry!" Madi said, still laughing. "Ally, put Gus in his cage," she said. She walked up to Michael and motioned for him to bend down so she could remove the feathers. Michael watched as Ally herded the bird in his cage, he could have sworn that Gus gave him an "I'll get you" look while climbing inside.

"He just needs to get used to you," Madi said, trying to make him feel better, but she knew that Gus just didn't like him.

Michael sat on the couch opposite the cage, trying to calm down. Madi sat on the chair next to him, still giggling inside.

"Hey, before I forget, we were invited to the neighborhood seafood broil tonight," he said. "Not together, everyone was invited. I mean, we can go together, they didn't ask us as a couple, but we could . . . I mean not a . . . you know." He got more tongue-tied as he spoke. *What's the matter with me? I'm not a teenager.*

Madi was smiling at his unarticulated scramble for words, not sure if he was nervous for asking or still dazed from the aerial attack. "We would love to go with you. What should we bring?"

"Nothing—it's an everyone-chip-in-the-tip-jar thing."

Ally put in the DVD, crawled into her mother's lap, and laid her head against the armrest. Michael watched Madi run her fingers through Ally's hair and twirl strands around her index finger. She caught him gazing and they locked eyes for a brief moment, and it seemed to be a standoff of who was going to smile first. But the sincerity of their shared gaze had more than a hint of flirting; for the first time they knew there was more there. A loud opening scene broke off the stare, and they settled into an animated story about a princess.

ം

The music became louder and caught the attention of Michael, who was disoriented with his whereabouts and blurry-eyed from waking up. He looked over at Madi to see her and Ally curled up with each other in the chair.

He shook Madi. "Hey, Madi. Wake up, we fell asleep," he said softly.

She opened her eyes and without moving smiled at Michael, which caught him off guard. She was happy he was still there.

"What time is it?" she asked.

Looking at his phone, he said, "It's five o'clock. I told them we would be there around six."

"We can do that," she said, untangling herself from Ally.

"I'm going to run back to the house and change. I'll be back over in forty-five minutes," he said.

Shutting the front door behind him, he saw the small storm had passed over while they were asleep. Lady was sitting on his front porch step patiently waiting for him.

After a quick shower and change of clothes, he walked back over to Madi's to find Ally outside digging a worm up from the flower bed. "Are you ready for some seafood?" he asked.

"I'd rather have chicken," she said.

"Well, maybe they'll have something you like."

Madi appeared wearing a light brown floral sundress and strappy flat shoes. She seemed to have a glow around her—Michael wasn't sure if it was because he hadn't had much sleep. Or maybe it was real. Her hair was down and her bangs had a slight curl, pulling them out of her eyes.

"Wow, you look beautiful," he said, letting his guard down.

She smiled a big Georgia smile. "Thank you," she said.

"Hey, one thing I failed to mention. That odor we smelled last night came from the couple who invited us." Madi looked at him funny. "Don't worry—it's not that kind of party," he said.

"Well, I know you wouldn't take us to that kind of party. I

am just wondering how you knew the couple," she said with a grin.

"Long story. I'll tell you when we are alone," he said.

I sure hope that is soon, she thought.

Chapter 20

Michael grimaced with all his strength during his last set and slammed the bar against the weight rack—he hadn't done any bench-pressing for years. Deanne tossed him a towel to wipe sweat from his face.

"You're doing better," she said.

He had been religiously going to the gym three times a week and running during the off days. Unfortunately, the starstruck Mrs. Hentise had figured out his schedule and made it a point to work out during those times. By now everyone on the island knew Michael Curry the world-renowned composer was staying the summer with them.

It was a few days before they had to leave for his first concert. He was excited Madi was going with him and hoped she would have a good experience, but he was a little worried about her reaction when he asked her to go. Gulping down a small Dixie cup of cool water, he walked the treadmill to cool down. *Right on time,* he thought, seeing Mrs. Hentise opening the door.

"I was wondering if you were going to make it today," he said.

"Oh yes, good day to work out," she said while blushing.

She and Mr. Hentise were health nuts and never missed a workout. For all the trouble of being whispered about, at least Michael had gotten a few good cooking tips from them.

"Anytime you guys want an evening to yourselves we would be happy to keep Ally," she said.

"Well, thank you, I'll keep that in mind. Madi and I are really just friends."

"Friends?" She rolled her eyes. It was a small island and the news of a celebrity being there was big, but so was young love.

"How's the new album coming?" she asked.

"Coming along well. I have a concert in a few days and I thought I would play a few new songs."

"Oh . . . where is your concert?"

"It's just north of here; we'll be gone for a few days," he replied.

"We? Must be more than friends," she grinned.

He just laughed, not knowing how to answer without being interrogated.

"I don't want to step out of bounds, but would you consider a concert here?" she pushed.

"Maybe. I'll have to think about that," he said. Michael didn't like turning people down if it benefited children or if they just liked his music. He wasn't a fan of people who would ask him to play, then make money off the evening.

Mrs. Hentise made her way to the treadmill beside Michael's. Deanne leaned over his treadmill and set it for twenty minutes. "I thought this was a cooldown? That looks more like a workout," he said, pointing to the settings.

She just smiled. Michael thought she must think him a lightweight.

Mrs. Hentise now had her cell phone out, showing him pictures of her family.

Hearing the door open, he looked up to see Madi entering. His first thought was *Where is Ally?* but his next was *Wow!* She wore short black aerobic pants with yellow stripes running down each side of her well-toned legs and a tight-fitting sleeveless shirt.

Knowing he was there, Madi first looked toward the weights

then to her left where she found him gazing at her from his contraption of torture, the treadmill. She gave him a warm and intimate smile followed by a soft hello.

His gut was beginning to hurt from a middle school crush. As he started to say hi back, Mrs. Hentise pushed her phone back in his face, causing him to lose sight of Madi. He looked around the iPhone toward Madi, expecting to see her cute little figure. Instead he found himself looking at the old tin-tiled ceiling. *Tin ceiling? Where did that come from, I don't . . .*

When he had tried to steal another peek at Madi, he'd stepped half on the side rail and half on the treadmill. His first reaction was to reach forward and grab the bar, but he only found a half-full water bottle in his hand.

Madi watched on in horror as this guy who seemed to be working hard to impress her looked like a drunk running from the police on a frozen lake. At first she could only stare in shock, then she reached toward him. "Michael!"

Deanne rounded the corner just in time to watch the final act of desperation as one leg shot through the handrail and the other kicked straight up. Somehow he managed to take the treadmill to the ground with him on his side. The belt never quit running and as Michael felt the heat on his backside, he arched his back to keep his butt off the evil machine that was trying to eat him.

Deanne squatted down and slammed her right hand against the stop button, causing the demon-possessed machine to stop its attack on Michael. Just as he looked back at Madi, whose face was buried in her hands, his half-full water bottle landed on his head.

"Are you okay?" the trainer said, doing her best to keep a straight face.

Before he could answer, he heard from the culprit on the neighboring treadmill. "Oh, you got to be careful on these contraptions."

Michael just bit his tongue.

Madi gripped Michael's wrist and pulled him up to his feet. Looking into his eyes, she could sense that the only thing really hurt was his pride. She asked anyway, "Are you sure you're okay?"

"Yeah, I'm fine," he replied, pulling his shorts back to their normal position.

Madi and Michael locked eyes; she couldn't hold it any longer and burst into a loud laugh. "I'm sorry, I don't mean to laugh," she said through her hands covering her face.

"Yeah, yeah. Laugh it up," he replied in frustration.

Tears welled up in her eyes as she fought back the gut-wrenching hysteria.

Looking back at Deanne, who was also wiping the tears out of her eyes, Michael said, "I'm cooled down!"

She only offered him a wave of agreement before turning back to her office, shoulders shaking in quiet laughter.

"I'm going to the store for more vegetables and fruit," he said.

"Do you want me to come?" Madi asked still giggling.

He opened the door and held it for her, motioning her to lead the way.

As soon as the door closed, low laughter and snickering shot through the entire gym, including Deanne's office.

Chapter 21

"Where is Ally?" Michael asked, sliding into the golf cart.

"I found a babysitter the other day. A teenager who is also staying here for the summer," she replied.

"That's helpful. Am I taking you away from working out?" he asked.

"Nah, I'll do some cardio later," she said. Madi loved everything about her little girl but appreciated the time apart.

Sliding to a stop in front of the grocery store, Michael noticed three elderly men sitting on an old church pew out front. They were carrying on a conversation about a fishing trip earlier that day, but the conversation stalled once Madi approached the door. Michael walked a few steps behind her, laughing inside at the men's expressions toward her workout attire.

Once she disappeared inside, Michael turned back toward the men. "She's hot, isn't she?" he said. Walking in he found her waiting for him just inside the door. *Oh crap! Did she hear that?* he thought.

Oh my gosh! He just called me hot! She sighed.

"What did he say?" one of the old men yelled at the other.

"I don't know, something about it being hot," another said.

"He didn't say anything about the weather; he said the girl was hot!"

The third man shouted, "Well, hell, maybe he ought to get her in the air-conditioning."

The third man just waved his hand toward the first man, and their conversation turned back to their fishing story.

"How long is your babysitter staying with Ally?" Michael asked.

"Just a few hours."

"Oh, okay," he replied.

"Why?" she questioned.

"Well, I would like to go eat somewhere tonight and thought it might be nice if it was just us."

"Just us?" she teased him, disappearing around a set of shelves.

He followed her into the bread aisle. "Yes, just us. What do you say?"

"Oh, I don't know, I'm not sure if I can date boys who can't ride treadmills." She smiled.

"Then you might need to be careful around me. Between getting my butt kicked by a bird, lying in chum bait, and falling off treadmills, I'm not the ideal guy to date."

She started laughing. "You have definitely been interesting."

"And aren't you the one who knocked over the bucket of bait?" he added. She just continued laughing while walking toward the snacks. *Please follow me!* she thought, loving the playful attention.

She turned around to see Michael gone. "Michael?" she blurted. She looked back toward the bread aisle and then to the fruit. *Where did he go?* She spun to the snack aisle to find him holding her favorite Goldfish snacks.

"Here." He handed her the box.

He's already learning me. Crap! I'm falling for him. Please let this be okay!

"Supper?" He hinted for a yes.

"Of course. I'm sure the babysitter doesn't mind staying."

"I hope the attack bird hasn't gotten her," he said, picking up a bag of chips.

"I'm sure she's okay." When Madi had left, Gus had been sitting on the babysitter's shoulder entertaining the girls with Hot Fries. She wondered why that bird hated Michael so much.

ꙮ

He pulled the golf cart up to Madi's front porch. "Where are you taking me tonight?" she asked.

"Randy's Bar and Grill. I hear they have great broiled shrimp and crawfish."

"So it's not a black-tie formal dress date?" She smiled.

"Shorts and flip-flops!" he teased back.

"I'll be ready in forty-five minutes." She grabbed her bags and jumped up on the porch. Michael saw Ally appear at the door; he waved and gave her a wink.

Michael dashed into the cottage, peeled off his shirt, and cracked open the hot water in the shower. He was just stepping out of his boxer briefs when he heard Lady barking at the back door. Knowing from her history she wasn't going to stop until he let her in, he snuck out of the bathroom and walked through the living room, hesitating before going on the screened back porch. Standing naked in the doorway, he thought, *No one is out. I'll be fine.* He tiptoed around his piano and opened the back door to find Lady patiently waiting on him.

As she cleared the door, he heard, "Nude beach! Right on, dude!" It was Webster and Sunshine.

"My, my!" Sunshine stared at Michael.

His eyes widened and his face turned a bright red as he covered himself with his hands and darted behind the piano. "Hey, guys. Didn't expect to see anyone but Lady." He paused. "Well, good seeing you. Gotta go." He tried to excuse himself back inside.

"It was good seeing you too, Michael!" Sunshine shouted as she watched his white bare butt disappear inside the cottage.

"You want to find somewhere?" she asked Webster, raising her eyebrows.

ꙮ

Michael clicked a radio app on his phone and turned it to his favorite station. The wireless speakers rang out with music from one of his favorite bands. The visibility was zero when he reentered the steamy bathroom, and after throwing a towel over the shower curtain rod, he slipped through the opening and into the foggy shower.

Standing under the hot water, he thought about Madi and that he might possibly be her first date since her late husband. *Gosh, she dated him in high school. I might be the second or third guy she's ever dated.*

ꙮ

While in the shower, Madi could hear Ally and the babysitter playing. She felt good that Ally adapted to her so quickly.

What am I going to wear to a bar and grill? Dress? Shorts? What color? Can't go white. Oh my gosh, this is a date! I haven't been on a date since Cole. Come to think of it, I haven't been on a date with anyone but Cole.

Chapter 22

Madi walked across the street to find Michael backing the golf cart out of the garage. "You sure like this thing. Have you driven your car any?" she asked.

"It's too fun to drive this around," he said.

She climbed in and sat, knowing that with her short shorts, sliding in wasn't going to happen.

"Hang on." He smiled and they accelerated to five miles per hour.

"Can I ask you a question that could possibly land me into the creeper category?" he asked.

"I can't imagine," she curiously said.

Michael thought about what he was going to ask; if he wanted to back out, he couldn't now. "You're a professional barrel racer."

"Yes," she said.

"I would think that if you hit a metal barrel going as fast as you do that it would leave scars," he cautiously said.

"But what if I was so good that I didn't hit barrels?" she joked back.

"Well, I guess . . . I just . . . I shouldn't have brought this up." He was embarrassed.

She thought it was cute the way he was trying to back out of the question.

"Coconut butter," she said softly.

"Oh, okay," he said with a nervous smile.

He's looking at my legs. The thought intoxicated her.

"Wait! Don't move," he instructed Madi, parking the golf cart in front of Randy's Bar and Grill. She gave him a puzzled look as he ran to her side of the cart. "Let me get your door for you," he said, acting silly.

She playfully punched his arm. "There are no doors."

The wooden stairs in front of them led up to the restaurant on stilts. Madi stopped at the base of the stairs; Michael turned to see why. She held her hand up for him to take it and he laughed. "Any professional barrel racer who has never hit a barrel shouldn't need help climbing twelve steps." He smiled back at her, taking her hand.

ᘓᘐ

The inside of Randy's looked like the inside of a western saloon met a scene from *Hook*. The light shown through the cracks on the wooden floor and the bar sprawled the length of the wall on the northern side. A large ship prop hung over the bar, and pirate paraphernalia littered the ceiling and walls. A redheaded man stood behind the bar talking with a young waitress. Michael overheard someone call him Randy.

Out of all the crazy décor throughout the restaurant, there was an upright piano sitting in the corner facing the unmatched tables. The young waitress pointed to an empty table and asked them to sit there.

"You should have worn your formal black dress," he joked.

"Hey, y'all, welcome this evening. What can I get you to drink?" the young waitress cheerfully said in a thick southern accent.

"Light beer," Madi answered.

"Going all formal." Michael nodded with a grin. "Two of

them please," he added before ordering shrimp and crab legs for them both.

Their view was probably the best on the island, and Michael scooted his chair to catch a glimpse of the last part of the sunset. Within minutes after they watched it disappear into the gulf, another waitress made her rounds lighting the antique lanterns on the tables, then dimming the overhead lights.

"Wow, this is nice," Madi said.

Michael watched the flicker from the lantern reflect off the tri-gold necklace that hung around Madi's neck; her purple, low-cut top displayed just enough of her cleavage to distract Michael.

"So tell me more about these magical hay fields you have back home," he said, realizing he'd been staring.

She took a sip from the longneck bottle. "They are beautiful, peaceful."

A loud bell rang out through the restaurant, halting their conversation. The man behind the bar yelled, "On the house!" Everyone cheered. Michael and Madi smiled at each other and joined in on the cheer. Soon the waitress dropped off two more beers.

"Tell me about touring. Do you fly everywhere or ride a bus?" Madi asked, turning the conversation on him.

"Depends. If it's a tour that has two or three shows a week, I'll ride a tour bus. If just two a month, I'll fly."

"That's got to be nice, riding the bus. I drive everywhere and it gets tiring," she said.

"Yeah, I can see that. It's nice but to be honest, it gets lonely on the road."

She paused and thought for a moment. "Why isn't there a Mrs. Curry? No girlfriends from the past?" Madi teased him with her interrogation.

"Just never met the right girl," he replied. A faint memory of Tessa popped into his head, but he quickly let it go.

"Well, being a star, you have to have groupies," she joked.

"I've had my share of groupies following me."

"Really?" she asked, shocked.

"Yep, all gray hair and dentures."

"I don't believe just elderly people like your music," she said.

He just smirked and cut his eyes.

"I like your music," she offered honestly. "I'll tell you what. Ally and I will be your groupies."

He smiled at the gesture. "You'll be the two best-looking girls I've ever had along for a trip." He was shocked to hear himself say that, but it was true. Maybe the beer was loosening him up a little.

She smiled as he watched her eyes dance in the light of the lantern. Michael found himself becoming hypnotized. This was something he hadn't anticipated—something he hadn't felt in a while—a real crush turning serious.

Two big platters of shrimp and crab legs landed on the table in front of them, breaking the trance he was floating into. Michael looked up to see the owner.

"I'm Randy. It's good to have you guys eating with us tonight," he said. Michael wasn't sure if that was how he talked to everyone or if he knew who he was. "I would never pressure anybody, but there's an old beat-up piano over there and I know everyone would be honored to hear you. But again, no pressure," Randy said, returning to the bar.

That answered Michael's questions. "Okay," Michael said.

After devouring their shrimp and crabs, both of them sat back, stuffed.

"Can I get you any dessert?" the young waitress asked.

"I thought that *was* dessert. It was delicious," Michael replied.

The young girl took their empty platters and returned with two more beers.

"Are you going to play?" Madi asked him.

"Only if you sit with me," he replied. And before she could answer, he guided her to a tall bar stool beside the piano.

He opened the cover and began playing a soft and slow melody. "What would you like to hear?" he asked Madi.

"Surprise me," she said in a flirting tone.

"Okay. This is something I've been working on." He began playing a piece that was so perfect and advanced that the old piano felt out of its league.

Madi immediately fell into a reverie and leaned on the old piano, feeling the vibrations of the strings, pounded by every note. She watched Michael as he closed his eyes and let his own masterpiece envelop him in magic. She knew that feeling—she had experienced it many times in the Alicia hay fields.

After striking the last note, he opened his eyes to the applause of the crowd and to what he couldn't describe in any number of words—a beautiful blonde sitting next to him with eyes full of love, what he'd been searching for his whole life.

"That was beautiful. What is it called?" she softly asked.

"I'm still working on the title," he answered with a bit of a lie. He knew the title and had decided to leave it as a surprise for the amusement park.

She leaned down toward him. *Is she going to kiss me?* he thought. Just has her lips were inches from his face, she stopped. His heart was pounding and he wasn't sure if he was supposed to finish the reach for their first kiss. With eyes locked he leaned in and she tilted her head to the side and whispered in his ear, "Thank you." Then she pulled back and sat patiently, waiting for the next song.

His heart swelled. There was more intimacy in that one whisper than in the weeks of time already spent together.

Chapter 23

Michael walked Lady down the beach toward the Hentises' house. The waves washed harmoniously ashore with a light wind pressing against his body. They entered Lady's yard to find Mr. Hentise working vigorously in his makeshift garden.

"I figured I'd walk Lady back down here. I'm going to be out of town for a few days," Michael said.

Mr. Hentise wiped the sweat off his forehead with the back of his arm, his hands black from the soil he was using. "That's what I heard, a concert."

"Yes, sir."

"Come here, girl." He leaned over, patting the side of his leg, Lady made her way over to him.

"My wife isn't getting in your way, is she?" he asked.

Michael smiled. "No, sir."

"I know she's a little pushy; just let me know." He went back to working on his garden.

On the walk back Michael heard his name being called; he looked toward the blue house set on stilts and didn't see anyone. Pressing on he heard his name again. This time something caught his eyes in the pine tree behind the house—Webster was sitting on a branch nearly twenty-five feet up in the tree.

"Webster? What are you doing?" Michael asked.

"Oh, just hanging out. What about you?" he answered.

Michael wasn't sure why the kooky old hippie was in the tree. "You okay?" he asked.

"Yeah, man, just getting away."

"Okay, have a good day," Michael said, clueless.

Before he could walk away, Sunshine walked out onto the deck. "Hello, Michael," she said in a lewd tone.

"Hi, Sunshine." Michael waved. He could feel his butt burning with the stares from her as he walked off.

ꙮ

He backed out of his garage and climbed out of his ML450 to discover Ally standing in the grass. "Are you ready?" he asked.

She giggled with excitement. "I am! In less than two hours we'll be riding the meanest roller coaster ever!"

He looked over at the bags on the front porch of Madi's cottage. *Is she taking all those bags?*

Madi walked out of the front door and waved toward them.

"Give me just a second and I'll be over there," Michael yelled across the street.

Michael continued closing down his cottage, giving it a final walk-through to ensure everything was in its place and spotless. He locked the front door and gave it a strong nudge to make sure the latch caught. He backed across the street and popped the hatchback, and before he could assist Madi, he felt his car bounce as she loaded their first big suitcase.

"We're only going to be gone for three days," he said.

Reaching for another bag, she smiled back. "You know girls can't travel light."

After loading all the bags, they walked back up on the front porch; right as they reached the front door a massive green blur blew past them and across the front yard.

"Ally!" Madi shouted.

A voice from inside replied, "I'm sorry, Mom. I was just saying bye."

"Help us catch him!" Madi shouted toward the house.

"Us?" Michael pointed at himself in a concerned voice.

"I'm sure he's used to you by now." She ran toward his front yard.

"No, I'm sure he's *not* used to me." He followed her.

"We can't leave until we catch him!" Madi frantically said.

Reaching the middle of the street, Gus soared over Michael's neighbor's house and toward the beach.

"I'll go around back, and you stay on this side of the house in case he flies back over," Madi ordered. Ally chased after her mother while Michael walked through the cottages' front yards, looking in the trees and bushes, praying that Madi would be the one to catch the green devil bird.

Ally reappeared around from his neighbor's house. "Did you see him?"

"No."

"He just flew back over here," she said, out of breath.

He looked toward the sky and the tops of the trees but didn't see him. *This bird hates me! First he attacks me, now he's making me late for my own show!*

He heard Madi shouting but couldn't make out what she was saying. Walking toward the beach he spotted Gus high in the air. "How in the world are we going to catch him?" he said.

Gus sailed downward in the vicinity of the beach, so Michael started jogging around the corner of a cottage when he ran smack-dab into Madi, knocking her to the ground.

"Oh my, I'm sorry." He quickly reached down to her.

"He came this way!" she exclaimed.

"No, I just saw him head toward the beach."

"You go that way and I'll circle back around," she said without giving him a chance to argue.

An hour later Madi's concern turned into fear with every passing minute and no sight of Gus. She met up with Michael on the beach. "I can't believe this," she said with tears in her eyes.

"We'll find him," Michael assured her.

"I'm going back to the house just to make sure he didn't go back," she replied.

"Okay, I'll keep looking." She vanished with Ally around the blue house on stilts.

"Hey, brother, why all the running?" Michael looked up to find Webster still sitting in the tree with a bird's-eye-view of the show that had just unfolded. Michael stopped and stared in awe. Sitting in Webster's lap was an out of breath and panting green parrot.

"We've been looking for him." Michael pointed at Gus.

"Oh, man, I'm sorry. I didn't know. He's been sitting here with me for a while now." Webster was petting the bird as if it was a dog. *How in the world is this hippie petting him? Is it only me Gus hates?*

"Hang on, brother, and I'll climb down," Webster said.

"Okay, but hold onto him!"

"Well . . . I'm not sure how I can do that." Webster spun on the branch and Gus jumped off his lap. In mid-fall Gus spread his wings and gained flight, aiming at the only tall structure on the beach—Michael.

As the wind picked up under Gus's feathers, Michael swore that Gus's eyes turned demon red and his beak opened wide, headed for his target.

Michael did the only thing that came to mind in that split second—he turned and ran, a high-pitched scream escaping his mouth. Now sprinting, he thought he would be out of range; but to his horror, Gus had caught his second wind and was in hot pursuit of the piano man. Michael maintained his speed and ran toward his cottage, hollering at Madi at the top of his lungs. Across the street and in her yard, Madi heard his screams. She panicked. Was he seriously hurt?

"What was that?" Sunshine asked, running out on the deck.

Webster was now on the ground. "That was your naked dude! Man, can he run. Look at him go," Webster replied.

"He sure has a high-pitched scream," she said.

"I bet it's because he's into music," Webster said in his hippie drawl.

Madi rounded his cottage in time to see everything unfold. Michael was running up the beach to the cottages with a green bird just inches behind him. *Oh my gosh! That bird hates him.*

"Michael!" she screamed as she watched him run past his cottage. He was so focused on outrunning the bird that he ran past his target. He cut back and ran toward Madi. Now his plans were to run past, hoping that the devil bird would be snatched out of the air. And once he passed her, she scooped Gus out of the air.

"I got you!" she yelled.

Ally came from around the house. "You caught him!"

"It's okay," Madi softly spoke to Gus as he panted.

She quickly walked past Michael, headed to her house and to Gus's cage. "Thanks." She smiled at Michael.

Michael fell to the ground, out of breath. *I hate that damn bird!*

Looking down the beach he could hear Webster yelling, "Right on, dude!" giving him a thumbs-up.

Chapter 24

"And we're off!" Michael said, excited to finally be on the road. They hadn't spent as much time chasing his nemesis around the beach as he first feared.

Madi brought along Ally's coloring book for their two-hour drive. She observed how clean his car was and thought that maybe he had just taken the plastic off the seats. *Give Ally and me the weekend and we'll have it messed up,* she thought. She admired the black Mercedes and liked the idea of seeing out with no one seeing in through the tinted windows.

Ally watched as the palm trees vanished and more pine trees took their place the farther they drove from the coast. She was accepting of Michael being around more and more, and though she loved being entertained by his silly actions, the few hugs he had given her felt warm and safe. She looked at her surroundings in the backseat—her own DVD screen, air-conditioning vents, and favorite stuffed animal. She took a deep breath, placed her hands behind her head, and leaned back for the two-hour drive.

"There is something we should talk about," Michael started.

"What's that?" Madi asked.

"Once we get there it's going to get chaotic. These people haven't seen me in a while and everyone seems to be in a hurry.

You guys will be with me most of the time. Just have fun," he said.

Madi reached over and patted his hand resting on the gearshift. "We'll be fine." Her hand cupped over his fist, and she allowed her fingers to intertwine his. She held on for only a second or two and pulled away in fear of little eyes in the backseat.

"Michael?" Ally suddenly asked.

"Yes?" he answered.

"Today's been pretty fun already. You looked funny running from Gus down the beach."

Madi's heart started pounding in fear of Michael being embarrassed even more than he already was. Looking at her through the rearview mirror, he smiled and said, "I'm glad I entertain you." He broke into a gentle laugh thinking that he had to have looked funny running from the bird.

Madi sighed with relief at his laughter. She didn't want someone else's bird to cause her to lose someone she was interested in.

"Girls, you have to admit the last two weeks have been fun, but I bet the next three days will be a blast!"

"I bet they will," Ally snapped back.

Michael's phone rang, and with the push of a button on the steering wheel, Robin's voice took the place of the music playing in the background. "Hey, where are you?" Robin asked.

"Just getting on the interstate. What's up?" he asked.

"Just odd for you to be late," she replied.

Madi sank in her seat with embarrassment. He tried to comfort her with a smile. "Oh, we had to chase something down," he said.

"Is she in the car with you? What . . . am I on speakerphone?"

"Yes and yep."

"Hi Madi, I'm looking forward to meeting you," Robin said.

"Hi Robin, me too."

"Okay, Madi and I will have time to get to know each other; you have a photo shoot today," Robin said.

"Okay, we'll be at the resort in thirty-five minutes. Bye, Robin," Michael said.

As the call ended, Robin thought, *If this girl thinks she's going to work her way into this, she's got another thing coming!*

"I'm sorry, I didn't mean for you to be late," Madi replied.

"Don't worry about it. I'm not late. You ready for roller coasters?" he asked Ally.

She smiled and nodded her head with excitement.

❦

As they turned into the resort and pulled into the parking lot, Madi's eyebrows drew up her forehead, and her mouth fell open. Waiting on them were two semitrucks with a painting of Michael's eyes peering over his aviator sunglasses and his hair falling in front of them. Parked beside them were two forty-five-foot custom motor coaches and a half-dozen black Expeditions with tinted windows.

"Is this all for you?" she asked, highly impressed.

"Yep, overkill isn't it?"

"I think I could get used to it," she replied.

Once the ML450 came to a stop, someone opened Michael's door.

"Hello, Mr. Curry, I'll take care of your vehicle and bags. Hello, ma'am," the young man said.

Michael wasn't fazed by the attention and motioned for Madi and Ally to follow. Leading them toward a couple—a proud-looking woman and a man in a wheelchair—

Michael turned to Madi. "This is Robin and Doug."

Robin, not waiting for introductions, said, "You're late."

"And this is the first time," he smiled.

Madi's stomach sank, knowing she was the reason.

Robin leaned past Michael and stretched out her hand. "Hi, I'm Robin."

Madi shook her hand. "Nice to meet you."

"Okay, let's go." Robin turned and headed toward the hotel.

"Hi, I'm Doug." Doug reached out and shook Madi's hand, interrupting Robin's orders.

"Hi, Doug." Madi seemed to draw up with a teenage shyness.

"Okay, guys, lots to talk about." Robin pushed everyone toward the resort's main entrance, giving instructions and orders. "We have reserved the top floor. Madi, you and Ally have the suite next to Michael's, and this is Lisa. She'll be able to answer anything if Michael and myself are not around," she said, pointing to a young intern.

"Answers?" Madi asked, confused.

"During the show," Michael answered.

"Now for a big question." Michael stopped the entourage. He turned and faced Madi and Ally. Madi froze, scared of what he was going to ask her; but to her surprise he drew his attention to Ally.

"How would you like to be part of the show?" he asked.

"Doing what?" she cocked her head.

"Dancing with the princess," he smiled.

Her eyes widened, followed by her innocent smile. "Yeah!" she exclaimed.

"Yes," Madi corrected her.

Michael winked at Madi.

Chapter 25

"Mom, someone's knocking," Ally shouted to the other room in their spacious five-star suite. She opened the door just as Madi rounded the corner to find Michael in the hallway of the resort.

"I know it's kinda dumpy," he said.

"Yeah, it's pretty ratty, but I guess it will do for a few days," she said, mimicking his sarcasm.

"This is really nice," she added.

"Well, are you girls ready?" he asked.

Ally wasn't waiting for him to ask twice, so she walked out into the hallway.

"Robin has us a car waiting. Do you need anything?" he asked Madi.

"I believe I'm good." She stepped out into the hallway next to her daughter.

Reaching the bottom floor the elevator doors opened to an energetic lobby with fans and reporters; flashes from cameras began popping randomly. The young intern and two larger men in suits awaited them in the foyer.

Madi was in shock at all the commotion and felt guilty that she wasn't aware of Michael's popularity. "Wow, this is insane," she shouted above the crowd.

"It's not always like this," the young intern said, encouraging them to make their way to the Expedition waiting outside the doors.

Michael took his time shaking hands and taking pictures with as many people as he could. The intern had a look of fear that if she didn't herd him into the car she'd lose her job.

"Don't worry, Robin knows I'm fashionably late. She always pads thirty extra minutes—just don't tell her I know," Michael said to the intern.

Pulling out, Madi noticed the rigs and motor coaches were gone. "Where did the convoy go?" she asked.

"They are probably setting up for tomorrow night's show," he said.

Michael's stardom hadn't been born overnight; his assiduous character had led to the success he was experiencing. Robin had put her time in too with booking him in every show she could find. It wasn't till his eighteenth birthday that their hard work paid off with the signing of a record deal in Nashville, Tennessee. Since then he had been on dozens of tours in the States, as well as Europe and Africa, and he had met many prominent people throughout the world. The greatest trait that drew people to him was his humility and compassion for orphans; most fans knew his story growing up in an orphanage and loved his support.

Another Expedition joined theirs, and they made their way to the VIP gate entrance. As they got out, two young ladies approached Madi and asked if she and Ally would follow them to rehearsal for the show. Madi looked at Michael for approval.

"It's okay, she'll have fun. I'll catch up to you," he said.

Michael, Robin, and Doug made their way to the photo shoot and to meet a young boy who had been chosen to spend time with Michael through a Wishing Program.

"You really haven't said much about her," Robin interjected.

"I don't know what to say," he replied.

Robin squinted her eyes and looked at his expression. She

could tell by his demeanor that he was falling in love. "You're not telling me everything." She poked for more information.

He just smiled.

"Leave the boy alone," Doug said.

Someone waved at Robin for her assistance. "We're not done with this conversation," she replied.

"You know how she is about girlfriends. You might have to make up something so she'll leave you alone," Doug said.

Michael stopped and looked down at him. "I like her, Doug. There's something about her."

"I can see that. It's been over a year since I've seen you truly happy."

ᘓᘐ

Across the set, the young choreographer was coaching Ally, and to Madi's surprise she seemed to pick everything up with one instruction. Another dancer standing next to Madi made the comment, "That little girl is a true natural. This dance isn't easy and she's breezing through it."

Madi was excited for Ally and beamed as she thought, *Today has truly been magical.* She still hadn't come down off the cloud she felt she was on. It was perplexing to her that only weeks ago their intention had been to go to a small island and rest, and now she found herself watching her little girl rehearse for a dance that would be a dream come true.

After a few short hours of rehearsing and everyone complimenting Ally on her natural dance skills, the young intern returned to lead them to Michael.

"How was the rehearsal?" she asked Ally.

"Fun! I can't wait," Ally said as they rounded the corner to the view of center stage. The sun was setting, and the lights reflecting off the stage made for a magical moment as Madi thought about her little girl dancing in front of thousands.

On the stage a large group of people gathered around a

piano as a little boy played a simple tune; Michael leaned over him playing a melody. Behind the piano the program's name was featured, along with the story of what was happening on stage. Madi stood in silence for a moment as she watched Michael help the little boy's dream come true—playing a mini concert in front of everyone.

"It's been a long time since I've seen that boy this happy," Doug said as he approached Madi.

"Wow, I don't have words to explain this," she said. "I'm glad to see the little boy happy too," she added with a sincere smile.

Doug paused for a moment. "I wasn't talking about the little boy."

Madi looked down at Doug as he smiled at her.

Chapter 26

"How did Ally do with the choreographers?" Michael asked Madi.

"You wouldn't believe it. She did great."

"We'll rehearse together in just a short bit, then head to ride some rides," he replied.

"This is really special. Why didn't you tell me you were doing this for that little boy?" she asked.

Michael shrugged his shoulders. "I don't know, he's really a great kid."

Ally came pouncing up to them.

"You ready to rehearse with me now?" Michael asked her.

"Yes!" A big smile formed across her face.

After rehearsing for an hour, Michael leaned over to Ally as she stood near. "You ready to go ride some roller coasters?"

"You bet! Now?" she asked.

Michael turned to Robin, who was engaged in a conversation with one of the park officials. "You guys want to go?"

"No, you guys go have fun; we'll catch up later," Robin said.

The night's magic took both Madi and Ally to a place in their hearts that they had not felt in over two years. They ended up back in front of center stage for the lights and fireworks, and the crowd swarmed in preparation for the show.

Midway through the light show Madi looked up at her little

girl sitting on Michael's shoulders and experienced a vivid moment of déjà vu—Ally on Cole's shoulders. She feared that their experiences these next few days would trigger emotions of Michael taking the place of Cole, but she felt at peace. She wrapped around Michael's right arm and drew herself close to him; something about this made her feel safe.

After the fireworks Ally was exhausted and fell asleep leaning on Michael. Madi reached down and scooped her into her arms.

"Do you want me to carry her?" Michael asked.

"No, I can; it won't be too long before I'm not able to do this anymore."

They made their way through the crowd to the young intern who was waiting for them at the Expeditions. "Mr. Curry, Mrs. Abbott gave me this to hand to you. It's your itinerary for tomorrow," she said.

Once they reached their suites, Michael held Madi's door open so she could carry Ally into the bedroom. Once she put her in her bed she walked back to where Michael was waiting.

"I can't express how thankful I am for you asking us here."

"We have a lot more to go," he replied. Standing in the foyer of Madi's suite, mixed emotions overcame Michael. *Do I kiss her good night? Where do I stand with her? Too soon?*

But he didn't have to think long.

Madi made the first move, wrapping her arms around his waist and placing her head on his chest. "Thank you," she said.

He held her tightly but didn't make any move to kiss her. Then he left for his suite.

Against the closed door, Madi stood and second-guessed her feelings again. *Dang! He didn't try to kiss me. Is this right? What is he feeling? Am I the right girl?*

ꕥ

The following morning Madi and Ally beat Michael to breakfast at the resort's restaurant, which overlooked the tropical pool.

Robin and Doug were already at the table. "Did you guys sleep well?" Robin asked.

"We did. This is all so much," Madi said.

"Well, I'm glad you're enjoying it. You, my dear, have a big day ahead of you." Robin spoke to Ally, who was too busy eyeing the buffet.

"Here's a plate." Robin handed her a white porcelain plate from the table.

"Where is Michael? I figured he'd be here by now," Madi said.

"Well, he's probably going through his show morning ritual," Robin said. "If you haven't noticed he's a bit type-A. He'll sleep in, get completely dressed, and never eat breakfast the morning of. Not sure why," Robin added.

Robin began eating her words when Michael showed up in workout clothes, and by the looks of the sweaty shirt, he'd just come from the gym.

"Good morning!" he said in a chipper tone.

"I'm going to catch up with Ally. Did you sleep well?" he asked Madi as he snatched a plate from the table.

Madi nodded her head yes and then looked back at Robin.

"You must have some impact on that boy," Robin said, smiling, though she was churning inside with the thought of Madi having any influence over Michael.

The entourage left the resort in the four black Expeditions and barreled their way to the park. Madi stepped out and noticed the two motor coaches parked close to the VIP entrance.

"I hope you don't mind sharing a bus with me today," Michael said.

She couldn't tell if he was being serious or sarcastic. "Well, I guess we'll manage."

The three of them stepped onto Michael's tour bus and Madi couldn't believe it. From granite countertops to mahogany wood paneling on the wall with mood lights shining from behind, it was everything first class stood for.

"Unfortunately this is home away from home," he said.

"Yeah, unfortunately." She still couldn't tell if he was serious.

Madi toured the bus and saw that one of the two rooms in the back had her and Ally's names on the door. *They haven't left out anything!*

Their day went by quickly with Ally's rehearsal and Michael prepping for the show. Just after he had his sound check they went to eat with the executives of the park.

Sitting at the round table with the VP of the amusement park, Madi kept an eye on Ally, praying her daughter would use her best table manners.

Michael leaned over to her. "You okay?" he asked.

"Yes." She smiled. "Why?"

"You seem uptight about something," he said.

"No, I'm fine." She lied. Four weeks ago she had been wondering what she was going to do with her lame horse, and now she was at a park, her daughter in the main show, being escorted everywhere, and now eating in a private room with the VP sitting next to her in his Armani suit. *Yes, I'm uptight!*

Ally was on her best behavior, but Madi was still watching. She reached for a package of crackers, and seeing her hand shaking she quickly drew it back. Everyone at the table started laughing at something the VP said; she didn't hear what he said but she laughed anyway to cover her nerves. She attempted to retrieve the package of crackers again but once again her hand shook.

Michael noticed her frustration and handed her the package, giving her a concerned look. *I'm okay. I'm okay. Just breathe.* She took a deep breath, forgetting she had just taken a bite of a cracker, and inhaled a tiny square of baked white bread.

At first she tried to hide the cough, but that only led to a minor choke. Then she tried pushing with her stomach muscles, which was a horrible idea. First it just lodged the cracker deeper in her throat. Second it built up a large gas bubble that almost surfaced from the rear.

"Are you okay?" Michael asked, noticing she was turning red. But she couldn't answer him; she needed water! She sprang up from her seat and reached for her glass of water, but the motion unleashed the giant gas bubble and she loudly passed gas!

That terrified her so badly that while putting the glass of ice water back, she lost it somewhere between the dessert spoon and salad fork. The glass finally fell in the VP's Armani-clad lap. The horror almost made her pass out. Michael just sat, speechless.

Doug came to her rescue, announcing that she was choking, and everyone jumped from their chairs. That night the little blonde rodeo girl from Georgia who didn't want to draw any attention to herself was the main act for supper.

After Michael got her some water and the VP dried off, everyone started to settle back down. Madi was horrified, and looking at Michael, she could tell he was about to explode. Once he lost the fight of holding his breath, he burst into an uncontrollable breathless laughter. Madi had no choice but to give in with him, and soon both were brought to tears.

"Michael! There's nothing funny about her choking." Doug was getting upset.

"If you knew the last three weeks we've had, you'd be laughing too!"

As everyone joined in, Madi's nerves were finally eased.

Gosh, what a crazy day! I sure am glad he has a sense of humor, Madi thought.

Chapter 27

The concert couldn't have come any sooner for Madi. She was still embarrassed but felt a little relieved from her conversation with the VP after the table incident.

The young intern escorted her and Ally to the dressing room. "If you like I will stay with her every minute if you would like to see the show from out front." Madi knew she'd only be a few feet from her and agreed to sit out front with Robin and Doug.

Madi walked back to the motor coach where a small group of men gathered at the door; one of them opened it for Madi. She smiled and stepped up to find Michael rolling his sleeves up. She paused once they locked eyes. His dark hair was teased up and he was wearing black slacks, a black leather belt, and a black button-down shirt that caught every angle of his arms and chest. He smiled at Madi, hypnotizing her. *Holy cow! This man is so handsome!*

"You okay?" Michael asked, seeing her expression change.

"I'm okay. You look great," she answered.

"Is Ally ready?"

"You can't image how excited she is about this," she said.

"I have twenty minutes before I go on; stay with me," he asked.

They sat at the table across from each other. "Madi, I'm not interested in rushing into anything between us," he started.

The words scared Madi. *Where is this going?*

"But I need to know if I'm going too far with you. I don't want to scare you off."

She smiled in relief. "I'm okay."

"It's not like me to . . . become interested in someone this fast. But I would like to see where it takes us."

Madi sat listening and biting her bottom lip. "I don't know what to say, but its okay." She hadn't spoken to any man about a relationship other than Cole.

A knock came from the front door. "Five minutes," a voice from the outside said.

Michael sat back and stretched his arms over his head. "Well, then, I have a surprise tonight," he said.

"I'm not dancing." She smiled.

"I'll let you know what the title of that song is that I played at the bar."

"What?" she asked.

"During the show."

Another knock. "Two minutes!"

He stood up and looked one more time in the mirror. "You ready?" he asked.

"Me? Yes."

They stepped out of the bus and while walking backstage he reached over without looking and held her hand. She let her fingers entwine his, and a school crush tingle overcame her body.

"Wish me luck," he said before stepping away from her.

Without letting go of his hand, she pulled him back to her, and standing on her tiptoes she she placed her lips on his. "Break a leg," she said, smiling.

For a moment he lost feeling in his body, and the surrounding noise of the crowd went mute. *Whoa,* he thought. Then with a smile, he stepped up on the stage to a huge roar of the crowd.

I hope I just didn't mess up, she thought, walking to her seat.

Michael walked up to the black baby grand piano that sat

center stage, and he waved to the sold-out crowd. Sitting down he closed his eyes and rubbed his hands, and with fingers on the keys he went into a strong melody. The lights began changing with the tone of his music. He played one song after another without pausing in between them. Then, after playing for ten minutes, he stopped and leaned back.

"Good evening. Thank you for coming out," he said into the microphone. The crowd broke into roaring applause.

"Since we are in the most magical place, I have a new song that I would like to play for you." He began playing a few notes. "I've only played this once for someone very special, so you will be the first crowd to hear it. I give you, 'Imaginational Magic!'" And he broke into the same song he had played for Madi at the bar just a few nights ago.

She couldn't believe her ears. *Imaginational Magic* . . . the same words she used to describe her fields back home in Georgia.

The musical piece flowed into the chorus, and dancers began entering the stage from somewhere behind the piano. They danced and twirled to every note Michael hit. As the piece elevated and the volume grew, four more dancers entered the stage with the princess and the little eight-year-old girl from Georgia. Madi cupped her mouth in shock at the motion and smoothness her little girl posed. As Ally twirled past her mother, she caught a glimpse and smiled at her, and Madi began to cry. Joyful tears ran down her face as the song that was inspired by the fields of Alicia, her little girl dancing, and this stranger that had brought happiness to her life entertained the crowd.

The musical piece became louder, three-dimensional characters beamed in the sky with lasers, fireworks exploded overhead, and Ally danced on stage. Michael hit the last note, and a large exhibit of fireworks exploded.

Ally was close to him and he caught her attention. "You, my

dear, were awesome and very beautiful," he shouted over the crackling above.

With a smile from ear to ear, she said, "I wish my dad could have seen me."

"He did. I promise, he did," Michael assured her.

Robin put her arm around Madi and drew her close with excitement of the show on stage. "What did you think?"

"Incredible!" Madi replied.

"I don't know what you said or did, but I wasn't sure we would get him back on stage after Tessa left him."

Madi's excitement faded into shock. At first she couldn't move, then she twisted her body to Robin. "Tessa?" she shouted over the crowd.

Robin was smiling. "Tessa, his fiancée!" she shouted. Then she realized Madi didn't know who Tessa was. Robin's facial expression changed immediately to one of surprise. "He didn't tell you?"

Madi shook her head no. She wasn't interested in hearing anymore.

As Madi walked away, Robin chuckled to herself. *Now you know.*

Chapter 28

Ally, shaking with excitement, jumped off the stage and into Madi's arms. Michael followed her down the steps, only to have Madi turn with Ally in her arms and walk off. *Huh. Not the reaction I was expecting*, he thought.

He tried to follow them to the motor coach, but fans with backstage access stopped him for autographs and pictures. Finally he excused himself and darted for the bus. Just then someone grabbed his arm and spun him around; it was Robin. "You did great!" she started.

"Give me a second. I need to see what's wrong with Madi," he responded, pulling away from Robin's grip.

"She'll be fine. I might have mentioned something," Robin replied.

Michael turned in concern. "What did you say?"

"I mentioned Tessa. I thought you would have talked to her about Tessa," Robin said.

"I wasn't quite ready," he said, taking a deep breath. "I better go talk to her."

"Let her be, she'll get over it," Robin said.

"No, I need to talk to her." His pace slowed as he walked to the bus, and reaching the door, he hesitated. Thinking back, he could see Tessa's face.

Tessa and Michael had met while he was on vacation with a

few friends in the Swiss Alps. She was with a group of college student interns from an education abroad program from the States. She had graduated from college with her bachelor's of science and was working on her grad program for teaching. Tessa caught Michael's eye while she was assisting a few girls with their lift passes. She had turned to walk toward the door when she physically ran into Michael.

She was tall and slim with straight, long, brown hair. She was extremely athletic and had a competitive side that would rival most professional athletes. Back in the ski lodge Michael found himself looking at a beautiful young lady in a white ski bib and dark coat, her hair pulled back in a thick headband to keep her ears warm.

"Oh, I'm sorry . . . here, let me help you with that," Tessa said as she picked up one of Michael's poles.

"It's okay. You're American?" he asked.

"Yes, we are here on an international program for future teachers," she volunteered.

"Ski teachers?" he joked.

"No, but that's one of the perks. Skiing every day," she said, laughing. Their conversation led to the lift chairs. Something about her hypnotized him and he couldn't see past her beauty, even though his friends commented more than once about how much of a witch they thought she was. With her rude and demanding attitude, she successfully ran them off and she had Michael to herself the rest of the trip. Tessa played a cool game of pretending not to know who he was, and Michael never suspected anything different.

Late last year Michael's friends had stayed on him about her demanding demeanor and spoiled attitude, and he began realizing she was using him for money and popularity. Convinced that he could change her, he asked her hand in marriage only to find things getting worse. She stopped visiting the orphanages and wouldn't have anything to do with his friends. Tessa became cold toward Michael and spent most of her time shopping.

It was during supper one night with Robin and Doug when all hell broke loose. Doug mentioned a prenuptial agreement and Tessa went off. She spouted off to Doug that it wasn't any of his damn business and to stay out of it. Michael's eyes were finally opened to the real Tessa—a conniving user.

After walking her out to the street, he collected the two-carat diamond ring and sent her into the New York City night and out of his life after dating for three years. What he never knew was that Robin and Tessa never lost contact of each other. The two similar-minded women had built a friendship that wasn't going to be interrupted by a breakup.

Now as Michael leaned on the motor coach, his thoughts raced. *I knew this was too good to be true. Just go in there and tell her you're sorry and take her home. Do I really need someone back at home while I'm on the road? Crap, what do I do?*

Michael entered the bus. "Robin told me she mentioned Tessa," he started.

Madi was coming from the back where he could hear Ally, still excited about the show.

"It's okay." She tried to ignore him.

"No, you're mad," he replied.

Looking back at him with fire in her eyes, she asked, "Who is Tessa?"

"Just someone from the past." He didn't want to answer the question.

"Fiancée is not just someone from the past! Why didn't you tell me?"

He stood there trying to gather his thoughts.

"By not telling me it means there are still feelings there." She took a deep breath. "I let you in my life and you blocked yours!"

Ally came running out from behind Madi. “That was awesome. I’m ready for the next one!” she exclaimed.

But before Michael could say anything Madi interrupted. “There’s not going to be a next time!” She grabbed Ally’s hand, and with her bag around her shoulder she muscled her way around Michael.

“Mom! Why are you mad? Did I do something?” Ally cried.

“No, sweetie, you did everything right. I am so proud of you. But we don’t belong here.” She walked off the bus.

Michael stumbled down the steps to chase after her. “Madi! I don’t think you understand,” he said.

Madi turned with tears in her eyes. “I do understand. I trusted you, Michael. You lied to me about there being someone else.”

“I didn’t lie. She is somebody from the past!” he shouted back. “You are blowing this out of proportion,” he added.

“Maybe I am, but I can’t be around someone who isn’t honest.”

By this time the young intern walked up.

“Can you find me a ride back to the resort?” Madi asked the confused intern.

Michael nodded for her to help and walked back to the bus. Just before stepping on he looked back to see Ally’s head lying on her mom’s shoulder staring back at him, confused.

“Mom, I don’t understand. Why are you mad at Michael?” Ally asked.

“He just wasn’t honest with me,” she answered. She stared into the darkness through the tinted windows of the black Expedition.

Michael arrived back at the resort an hour later to find that Madi had checked out and rented a car. *Wow, this is so messed up.* He sat in the lobby for hours trying to gather his thoughts of what to do.

Finally Doug showed up. “Why don’t you get some rest and we’ll figure it out together tomorrow?” he said to Michael.

"I don't know what I did. I mean, I guess I should have told her about Tessa, but there's nothing there anymore."

"You know that, but does Madi?" Doug replied. "It's obvious that both of you have had your pain; give her some time and then sit down with her."

Without responding, Michael made his way up to his suite and fell asleep, lying crossways on the bed with his clothes still on.

Chapter 29

The rental car swerved on the dark interstate as Madi dialed her father's cell phone. After several rings his recorded voice answered, instructing the caller to leave a message.

"Dad, Ally and I are heading home for a bit." She hung up.

"Mom, who's going to feed Gus?" Ally asked. She hadn't said much since they had left.

"I'll get your babysitter to. Gus likes her."

She texted Lenny, the babysitter, and got an instant reply "yes."

After stopping only twice for fuel and food they pulled up to the farm just after midnight.

Madi and Ally woke up to the fresh smell of breakfast and coffee. The sunlight coming through the window shades blinded Madi as she stumbled to put on a pair of shorts. Wandering out onto the hallway's wooden floors, she bumped into her mom.

"Are you okay?"

"Yes, I will be after coffee."

Her father was sitting reading the morning paper, coffee cooling on the Formica table that they'd had since Madi was a little girl.

"Well, good morning!" His voice was warming and welcoming to Madi's ears.

"Hey, Dad."

"You come home to check on Bay?" he asked, regaining his place in the paper.

"Among other things." She blew on her cup and looked out the window at Bay and Grey grazing beyond one of the fields.

"You must really like him," his voice picked up from behind the paper.

"No, and I really don't want to talk about it," she tried saying in a polite voice.

He knew his little girl and sensed her emotions toward this new man, but he didn't press the issue.

Madi carried her cup and made her way to the front porch, settling into their white wicker porch swing. She pulled her knees to her chest and cuddled close to the steaming cup. A few minutes later her father walked out the front door.

"Going to the feed store," he said, standing in place waiting for an answer.

"Okay?" Madi said.

"No, I mean we are going to the feed store," he demanded.

She wasn't going to argue, and after she changed clothes she climbed in the truck that was waiting for her.

As they pulled out onto the highway she glanced back at the white dust that hovered above the long gravel road. She didn't want to have this conversation. Not today.

"Start from the beginning," her father said.

She knew that he was interested in helping, so she began. "It's not a long story," she said. And for their brief trip to town she explained their story and last night's events.

James turned off the truck after backing up to the concrete ramp behind the feed store. Then he looked his little girl in the eye. "What is the issue? He didn't want to tell you about his ex. Kiddo, you wouldn't talk about Cole for well over a year and a half. Whose pain are we dealing with here? He's obviously interested in you. Why else would he not tell you about someone who hurt him in the past?"

Madi tried to interrupt.

"No, hang on. Sweetie, you've dated one man your whole life, and maybe this guy isn't the guy, but you need to understand that most men are driven by their hearts. Remember, their identity will be determined by their activity."

His words penetrated deep, and she sat in silence while he got out and helped load his feed. Madi didn't say a word on the way home; she kept thinking about identity. Michael was so giving, both with money and time, and he was so compassionate with others. *His activities? What does that even mean?*

As the truck came to a stop at the farm and the dust cleared, James looked over at Madi. He couldn't help but imagine her in coveralls and pigtails and eight years old again; he fought to let his little girl grow up. "You okay?" he asked.

She shook her head. "I will be. Tell mom and Ally I'll be a few minutes."

She climbed through the white three-rail fence that led to her favorite place in the world, her dad's first Bermuda field. The field hadn't been cut in weeks due to rain; the grass came up to her waist and as she walked through it, she held out her hand to glide her palm across the tips of the green stalks. Sitting down in the field she disappeared into the sea of grass. The wind had picked up and the sun was close to being directly above her. Lying back the grass folded over her body, making a hole in the field that could only be seen from the sky.

Madi took a deep breath and tried to vanish into the world of imaginational magic, but for the first time in her life she couldn't leave the field. Once again she closed her eyes and felt the warm sunshine beaming down, but again she wasn't able to enter her world of imagination.

A voice spooked her; she sat up quickly but found nobody near. Closing her eyes once again, she heard the voice, this time calling her name. She stood again and looked around—no one. But something was different. Even though she hadn't wandered far from the barns and house, they were not anywhere in sight. In fact, she saw nothing but grass in every direction. *Am I losing my mind?*

She watched as the wind bullied its way through the field, pushing the grass in different directions, reminding her of the ocean behind Michael's cottage. Then in the distance she saw something that left her breathless. Her heart began to pound uncontrollably and she became scared. She surveyed the area looking for the quickest way out—the person approaching her looked too much like someone she knew all too well, and this was becoming a cruel joke. But she knew it was real when the sound of his voice reached her ears. *Cole!*

She wanted so badly to run and jump into his arms, but her legs became heavy as weights and she fell to her knees in tears. She held her hands over her mouth in shock, hyperventilating amidst the sobbing.

"Breathe, it's okay. Breathe." His voice was as calming as his glowing face. His appearance was as sharp as she remembered him; he was toned and his skin had a soft warm color that made his eyes a mesmerizing display. She could feel one hand on her shoulder and the other holding her left hand.

"Cole! You're here," she cried.

"I've always been here." He wrapped his arms around her and pulled her in tight. She could feel his heart beating and together they fell and disappeared into the sea of grass.

She lay with her head against his chest; his fingers ran through her hair, just like he'd done hundreds of times before.

"Is this heaven? Please tell me I've died and we're together again . . . this time forever," her voice shook.

"Heaven is beautiful, Madi. I can't describe it—the colors,

the sounds, and the people. You will see it one day. But this isn't heaven. This is your imaginational magical world."

"For the first time . . . it's disappointing. I want this to last," she wept.

"And it will, just not with me." His voice vibrated through his chest.

Madi sat up. "Not with you?" she asked.

Cole stood, took both her hands, and pulled her to her feet. "He's the right man, Madi. He will make you happy."

The tears began falling again. "You are the only man," she cried.

"I was, but search your heart, Madi. He's there. I want you to be happy. I want my little girl to be happy. Please don't let my memory steal that away from both of you. That's not how I want to be remembered."

Then the dam burst and Madi cried uncontrollably; it was as though she had to say good-bye all over again. For a few moments they stood together and Cole held her face with his warm hands. "You'll always be the one; you will always live in my heart. You are my treasure. Please be happy . . . for me and you." As he stepped back from her, his figure started fading into the windblown field. "I'm always here." And then he was gone.

Madi fell to her knees, heartbroken and numb. For a brief moment she thought it had been her imagination all along, until she heard a soft, small voice from behind.

"Mom?" She turned to find Ally.

"Hey, kiddo."

Ally looked around her. "Was that Daddy?"

Madi stood up, took a deep breath, and pulled her little girl close—in shock at the words she just heard. *Was that Daddy?* The words repeated over and over until Ally asked again.

"Mom?"

"Yes, sweetie, that was Daddy. He'll always be with us, and anytime you need him you'll find him here." She held the little girl's hand and walked back to the barns. Looking down at Ally, she thought, *She has her father's eyes.*

Madi paused at the white fence, her heartbeat finally calming in her chest. Turning back to the field one more time, she thought the words, *Thank you. I love you!*

Chapter 30

"I take it you found what you were searching for?" Madi's father asked while holding the trunk open for her.

"It's funny that one can get so much from home," she replied.

Looking at over the fields, he said, "Oh, I don't know. These fields have a way of teaching us about life."

"Yes they do." Madi smiled.

"So, when will we get to meet this music man?"

"I don't know; we have some talking to do. He might not be interested after the other night."

"He doesn't sound like the type that would let one evening determine his life."

Madi's mom and Ally walked out of the house; Ally was eating snacks out of a paper bag.

"I'm sorry this was such a quick trip," she apologized to her mother.

"Sometimes we need them. Bring this little girl back soon," she replied.

After hugging her parents she shut the car door and drove down the gravel drive. Bay stood at the fence as if saying good-bye.

She stopped at the end of the drive and faced Ally. "Are you ready to head back and see Gus?"

"And Michael and Lady," Ally said.

Madi smiled. "Me too." *If he'll have anything to do with me.*

ୡ

After a short four-hour trip, Madi pulled into the drive of her cottage. Michael's car was parked in his drive. It looked as though he had just returned too.

After unloading her bags she walked out on the front porch. It was killing her to talk with Michael; not being patient she made her way across the street. Creeping up the drive she watched the windows to see if she could see him. Then quietly stepping up the wooden steps, she glanced through the glass on the door.

A loud, low bark sent chills up her spine and caused her to leap forward. "Lady! Shhh . . . you scared me," she whispered, clutching her chest.

"No need to whisper—she's going to keep barking," Michael said, standing beside his car.

Madi stood in embarrassment on the front porch; she wasn't sure what to say. "I'm sorry, I was wondering if you had made it home," she replied.

He pointed at his car. "Yeah."

She felt foolish for asking such a dense question. "Okay."

He opened the back of the car and unloaded a few bags.

"Well, I'm glad you're home safe," she said, walking back toward her cottage.

He looked over his shoulder at her as she stepped out onto the street. Part of him wanted to let her go, but his gut said something else.

"Madi!" he yelled.

She stopped in the street and turned to face him.

"I'm sorry for not mentioning Tessa. I didn't think it would matter."

"I'm sorry I overreacted. It just seemed like you were keeping a secret." Madi could see the Hentises up the street on their daily run; not wanting to alert them to a disagreement, she moved toward Michael.

They waved as they jogged by. "Hey, guys, how was the concert?" Mrs. Hentise asked.

"It was good," Madi said.

"We are having a shrimp boil tomorrow for the Wellmans' return. Bring some wine," Mr. Hentise said, running backward.

"Who?" Madi asked.

"The Wellmans. I didn't know they were gone," he said. "You bite that wiener dog if it comes over," he said pointing to Lady, but she just made a moaning noise.

"Where's Ally?" he asked.

"Lenny, the babysitter, and she are playing with your favorite animal," she smiled, trying to break the tension.

Michael rolled his eyes.

She stepped closer. "Michael . . . I'm sorry," she spoke softly.

"Bring that bag with you," he said, pointing to the smaller bag on the drive.

She threw the strap over her shoulders and followed him inside. Closing the door behind her she had barely turned around when she felt his arms wrap around her body. The bag she was carrying hit the floor as she was swept off her feet.

Michael was worried about taking a chance, but he couldn't hold back anymore—and now with Madi wrapped in his arms and not fighting him, he knew his gamble had worked. Madi's feet dangled inches from the wooden floor as Michael held her up in his arms with their mouths locked together. She hadn't been kissed like that in years, and at this moment she was tingling all over and her heart was racing. Michael reached under her thighs and pulled her up higher on him. She wrapped her legs around his waist and he walked toward the couch without breaking their embrace.

Feeling her back pressing on the couch, Madi unwrapped her legs and laid back as he settled over her. She gently ran her fingers through his dark hair while enjoying the feeling of passion between them. Michael placed both thumbs under her chin and raised her head to kiss her neck. Moving her head to the side he playfully kissed below her ear, working his way up to her earlobe. The moisture from his lips shot ripples of desire through her spine, and her breath became heavier and heavier.

He worked his way around her neck and back to her lips; the excitement of it caused Madi's heart to skip a beat. He unbuttoned her long-sleeved shirt and pulled it off, revealing her tank top.

Repositioning herself on the couch, her hair flung out and landed over the armrest. She ran her fingers down his back as he kissed her neck; she pulled at his shoulders to bring his lips back onto hers. In one motion she ripped off his T-shirt and the warmth of his chest sent the same pain back up her spine.

The moment was catching up to her, but the sensation of luring eyes began to weigh on her conscience. She looked over toward the floor, and what she saw made her burst out in laughter.

Michael raised up and gave her a funny look. "I'm sorry," she giggled. He caught the same sight—a basset hound sitting quietly next to the couch with Madi's shirt dangling off her head.

Michael picked his shirt up and covered Lady's head completely. Without a sound, Lady laid down with her head between her front paws, still staring up at them through the fabric.

"This feels right. But maybe not just yet," Madi whispered in his ear.

He gently kissed her lips and then teased her neck with one last final kiss.

She grabbed his face with both hands. "Let's ease into this." She smiled, kissed him, then collected her shirt and made her way to the bathroom.

Michael was sitting on the couch catching his breath. “You happy?” he asked Lady. She sat up and gave him a loud bark, running to the back door.

“Really! You just wanted to go out!?”

Chapter 31

Michael grabbed the bottle of wine he had picked up earlier in the day while out with Madi. As he walked across the street he could see the sun setting through the trees and over a cottage farther down the street.

After knocking on Madi's door, Ally opened it with Gus sitting on her shoulder. "Hi, Michael," she said.

Michael didn't hear her; he was too focused on staring down the green devil bird. Gus crouched, squinted his eyes, and growled at Michael.

"It baffles me that he dislikes you that much," Madi said from down the hall. "Ally, go put him in his cage and put your shoes on," she added.

Michael waited until the coast was clear and then entered.

"I feel funny not knowing these people," Madi said.

"Oh, don't worry about it, small island, everyone is invited."

Madi sat down on the couch to put her shoes on.

"You ready?" he asked.

"Yep."

He closed the door behind them.

"Wait up a minute," he said. Both girls paused. "I found something today that seemed to fit you," he said to Madi. He pulled a small box out of the pocket of his rust-colored shorts and handed it to Madi.

"Why did you buy me something?" she said, opening the box.

Inside she found an aquamarine leather bracelet with a silver anchor to attach the ends together. Surprised, she looked back up at him. "I love it." She wrapped it around her wrist.

"It's called the anchor of hope. I thought you would like it," he said.

"Thank you." She hugged him, and Ally started off the porch.

"Wait up, Ally. I got you something too," he said.

She quickly spun around with a big, curious smile. He handed her a similar box; she quickly took the top off and dropped it to the ground. She pulled out a peach-colored leather bracelet with an atlas on it. "You have the whole world in front of you," he said.

She turned to Madi. "Thank you, Michael! Mom, put it on me, please."

Walking to the Hentises', Michael and Madi held hands while Ally walked in front of them and looked at her bracelet.

"Thank you," Madi said.

"I thought they fit you guys," he said.

"No, I mean thank you for putting up with my stupid nonsense. And taking—"

He interrupted her. "We are putting all that past us and moving on. Did you like the song Ally danced to?" he asked.

"No, not really," she answered. He was quiet for a short moment. "Of course I liked it!" She smiled.

Peepee dog met them in the front yard. "Mom, look! A wiener dog!" Ally said.

"His name is Amos, or he is better known as peepee dog," Michael said.

Madi gave him a funny look then remembered the statement he had made yesterday to Lady. "I take it you two know each other," she said.

"Hey, the piano man made it. Right on, dude." Webster gave Michael a high five.

"And you got clothes on this time. Righteous!" he added with his hippie flair.

Sunshine met them on the back porch. "Hi, Michael." She batted her eyes at him and gave him a big wink.

Madi looked up him. "You've made quite the impression with these people."

"You have no idea," he said under his breath.

Arriving at the party, Mrs. Hentise grabbed Madi by the right hand. "Come with me. Dear. You have to meet the Wellmans."

Madi looked back at Michael and smiled as she was escorted off.

"Here, this goes good with shrimp . . . and everything else." Mr. Hentise handed Michael a beer.

Michael walked up with him into a group of men carrying on a conversation about a storm heading their direction. He listened curiously; he had never been in a tropical storm and wondered if he would have to leave.

He asked Mr. Hentise about it. "Nah, it's a small storm with very little storm surge. If it was a category 2 or better then I would leave," he told Michael.

"You'll have to go to the island pier when it starts to come in. The waves will be big," another man told him.

Lenny walked up and started talking with Ally. They wandered off onto the beach with Amos hot on their trail. Michael noticed Madi standing with a group of women; she caught him looking on and smiled back at him. He raised his beer and pointed to the men talking about weather, and she raised her glass of wine and pointed at the ladies talking about the men talking about the weather. They laughed together.

They all rejoined on the back porch and gathered around two large tables. One man poured a tin basket of shrimp, crawfish, blue crabs, and potatoes in the center of the table.

"I need a beer!" Madi whispered to Michael. He opened one for her and handed it to her; all the other ladies were drinking wine but she didn't care. Her dad always said boiled seafood goes with a beer.

After everyone had eaten and the party started breaking up, Lenny asked Madi if she and Ally could go see Gus.

"Of course. Michael and I will walk back on the beach. We'll be there in thirty minutes." she told Lenny.

"Take your time. I have nothing to do," Lenny said.

"An hour?" Madi answered. Lenny smiled.

They walked up the road, the street lamps reflecting off the blacktop pavement. Then followed a path between two cottages and started back down the beach toward Michael's. They held hands as she talked about visiting her parents, but not mentioning anything about her experience in the fields.

"Would you like to see the farm?" she asked.

"I would," he replied.

Oh my gosh! Did I just ask that? Am I taking him home to meet my parents? She felt like a middle-school kid.

They strolled past the Hentises' house where a few people were still sitting on the porch. The beach was dark as they slipped by unnoticed. Or so they thought.

"You smell that?" she asked him.

"Yep. Must be . . ."

"What's up, young people?" Webster and Sunshine were sitting together in the darkness of the beach.

"Hey, guys, have a good night," Michael said.

"Oh, we will," a female voice replied from the dark beside her hippie man.

Madi and Michael giggled as they sped up their walk.

Stopping behind Michael's house, they sat on the beach to see what they could of the waves crashing on the beach. The moon was hidden and light was scarce.

"Would you like to come listen to something I've been working on?" he asked.

"Yes." She softly accepted his invention.

They entered the back porch and Michael sat down on the

leather bench. Madi sat next to him, and he began playing a soft melody.

After a few minutes of the composition, he asked, "What do you think?"

"Beautiful," she replied.

"Here is the whole song." And he played on.

She leaned her head on his shoulder and wrapped her arms around him. Little did she know what the song was titled.

Chapter 32

The next day, as Michael walked out of the gym, the wind almost blew the door out of his hand. Madi turned her back to the wind that was kicking up sand and spraying them violently.

"Wow! This came up fast," she said. The golf cart wasn't much protection for them as they skipped the store and headed back to check on Ally and Lenny. Madi had been through her share of storms but had never experienced a tropical storm. She was nervous with her only knowledge coming from the media. Michael on the other hand had never really been through a strong thunderstorm; his attitude was a little naive.

"Maybe we should let Gus out," Michael said, joking with Madi.

"That's not funny."

A yellow truck turned the corner with three or four surfboards sticking out of the back. Michael swerved out of their way.

"Whoa! That was close," Madi screamed.

"Just a bunch of young bucks," Michael replied. His patience was clearly well developed and his laid-back attitude contributed to the dismissal of almost being run over. He noticed they stopped near the island pier. "I bet Ally would like to see them surf," Michael said.

Pulling up to Madi's cottage they found the girls outside playing in the wind. "Looking for Gus?" Michael shouted. They looked confused at his picking question.

"Michael!" Madi said.

"You girls want to go watch some guys surf by the pier?" Michael asked.

"Sure," Ally replied.

"Let me text my mom," Lenny said. Madi came back out of the cottage with a light pink jacket and Ally's shoes. Lenny climbed on the backseat of the golf cart after getting permission to go. The girls squealed as Michael spun the tires in the gravel.

They could hear the roar of the thunderous waves before they pulled up to the pier. The noise was deafening as they yelled to each other. The moisture of the salt water filled the air. Ally walked behind Michael and Madi, intimidated by the raging surf.

"It's okay," Michael assured her.

Two of the four surfers sat on the tailgate of their truck watching the more experienced surfers tackle the enormous waves.

The waves were collapsing over the end of the pier, and a few people that were playing on the pier ran from every wave that came. Michael didn't hesitate to make his way to the pier.

"Michael, is that safe?" Madi asked.

"Yeah, I'm not going to the end," he said.

The three of them followed him as he stopped only a quarter of the way down the pier. They leaned on the railing and watched the two surfers ride their selected waves.

"That looks like fun," Ally said.

"We will have to rent a few boards and surf," Michael said.

"You know how?" she asked.

"Yep, and it is fun," he said.

The waterline was normally five to six feet below the pier, but the rough surf had raised it to only two or three feet below the concrete walkway. Every few waves that came rushing by splashed upon the pier and drizzled the four of them.

"I bet if we leaned out far enough we could splash a wave back," Ally said.

"You might if you could reach them," Madi replied, not thinking that Ally was taking her seriously.

An older couple walked out halfway onto the pier, not attempting to go any farther. Catching Madi's attention, the lady asked if she would take their picture. Madi took their camera and focused in on them as they posed against the opposite railing. Michael and Lenny watched as Madi instructed them to scoot closer to one of the lampposts on the pier. Just as Madi snapped the second picture she noticed the man's expression suddenly change. She lowered the camera. The man couldn't speak fast enough and pointed to something behind them. Madi turned to the railing and breaking waves behind her when she heard the horrifying words come from the man: "She's gone!"

Madi turned back to the man thinking, *Who's gone?* Still not understanding the couple's shock, she heard the man repeat the words, "The little girl!"

Madi spun and looked back at the vacant spot, then spun around looking for Ally. She was gone.

"Ally!" Madi screamed.

Ally had been watching as her mom took the couple's photo. She had heard one of the surfers yell, then turned around to see two surfers riding a wave and raising their fists, hollering out of excitement at the big wave they just caught.

Ally wondered if she could slap a wave as it passed by. At first she reached out through the railing but came up short, so she climbed over the railing and reached out, still too short. Holding on with her left hand she stretched as far as she could, but looking back at her hand she could see her fingertips sliding over the top. She lost her grip before she could even call for help.

As she fell she began to scream, but the next big wave

engulfed her and crashed down. She clawed to the surface and took a gasping breath, only to have another wave slam her into the concrete piling under the pier. She felt the pain quickly radiate through her head and neck, then down to her back as her sight faded into darkness.

Chapter 33

The world stopped moving. Madi's vision became gray. Everything from the last eight years flashed in front of her. *Oh, dear God, no!*

Michael leaned over the railing and surveyed the surf, looking for any sign of life. When Lenny screamed, everyone on the pier knew something terrible had just taken place. Michael jumped over the railing and grabbed the lower part of the bars to lean out farther, trying his best to look under the pier. Nothing. The elderly lady that Madi had photographed quickly removed her phone from her pocket and franticly dialed 911.

Madi stood paralyzed, not making a sound. Then in a flash, her instincts propelled her over the railing to rescue her only child. Michael grabbed her arm; looking into her eyes he knew she was going in the water.

"Get back over!" he demanded.

She didn't say a word, nor did she climb back over.

Lenny, thinking quickly, hollered at the surfers; the two who sat on the tailgate of the truck ran over while the others paddled over on their boards.

Michael and Madi exchanged looks, then both plunged into the violent surf.

This is a bad idea, Michael thought, as he knew he was the best swimmer.

Madi didn't expect the water to be so fierce and powerful. She held onto the side of the pier and kicked intensely with her shoes still on. Michael promptly discovered that his shoes were hindering him from any swimming progress, and releasing the pier, he pulled them off and let them go with the surf.

Visions flashed through Madi's mind of when Ally was born to the first time she learned to walk. Pictures of Cole and Madi paraded through her thoughts.

Cole, I need you. Please help us save our baby girl! Cole, please help. Don't let her die, I can't lose you both. God! Please save my little girl.

Madi began to panic. She felt herself hyperventilating and kicked to keep her head above the water. Then a large wave crashed down on top of her, and she could feel the salt water enter her lungs. *Oh, God . . . I'm not going to make it!*

The wave pushed her down; she could feel the current forcing her through the concrete pilings under the pier. Her blurry sight began to fade, and just before she lost consciousness, she saw Ally's lifeless body pressed against a piling—her arms held out as if begging to be rescued. *No! Ally, no!*

As the surfers gained control of their boards one surfer held the other's board as he dove under for Madi, who had just gone under. Michael submerged from behind on of the concrete pilings, finding it easier to navigate from behind.

He heard the surfer yell, "She went down here!"

Thinking they were talking about Ally, Michael took a deep breath and pulled himself under with the piling. As he kicked downward and away from the pier, he caught a glimpse of the surfer's feet. Michael pulled himself deeper, feeling the relief from the violent surf. The current was strong and as he started on his ascent to the surface for a breath, he saw the brown hair coming from behind one of the pilings.

Michael kicked as hard as he could to reach her. Feeling his breath begin to leave him, he pushed forward. Not wasting any time, he grabbed one of her arms that was extending out and shot to the surface. Breaking into the brutal surf, he gasped for breath and then called out, "I've got her!"

The answer was not what he expected. "Who? The girl or the lady?" *Lady? What lady? Where is Madi?*

He had no choice but to rely on the surfers to get Madi. He kicked as hard as he could to the beach. A crowd awaited him, and before he could touch bottom, a group of men peeled Ally out of his hands and another pulled him to shore. Michael watched as a lady performed CPR on the lifeless little girl. *God, not yet. It can't be her time.* He struggled to catch his breath as he watched on—the lady's expression turning to one of doom.

Hearing the commotion from behind him he turned to see another man carrying Madi out of the surf. Her body was limp, with no sign of life. The man fell to the sand when others took her out of his arms. Michael felt as though he was living in a dream. *This can't be happening.*

Then Madi gave a loud cough and gagged. "Thank God!" one of the men said, standing over her.

She turned, spitting out salt water, and locked eyes with Michael. She followed his sight as he turned back toward Ally, Madi screamed for her little girl. She couldn't feel her legs, and all strength had left her body, but she was hell-bent on getting to Ally. She began to crawl, when the same man who had saved her helped her to the body of her little girl. Michael fell to his knees beside Madi as she held Ally's lifeless hand, begging for God to give her back.

The lady administrating CPR wasn't letting up, but Michael could tell by her face that she felt it was too late. Madi cried uncontrollably. Michael put his arm around her, but she never felt it or even knew that he was beside her. Her world had stopped.

Then Ally gave a cough and a violent jerk. The lady quickly turned Ally onto her side and let the salt water escape from her lungs as more coughing followed. Madi embraced her, crying, "I thought I had lost you! You're okay now. I'm here. I'm here."

Ally began crying.

"Thank you, God. Thank you!" Michael prayed out loud.

Chapter 34

One of the surfers gave Michael a beach towel to wrap around Ally. He picked her up and carried her toward the golf cart.

"Thank you," Michael told the lady who had given her CPR. Madi walked quickly beside them, talking to Ally and comforting her.

The local first responder showed up in a small red truck with a flashing LED light on the dash. He met them halfway, carrying a black EMS bag.

"We should probably get her to the hospital," Michael told the young guy.

"Well, there's a problem. The bridge coming into the island was just washed away. No one's coming or going," the young first responder said.

"Really? This weather is not bad enough to knock out a bridge," another man said.

"I know. But we can get her in a boat and go up to the next boat launch," the young guy suggested.

"No! We are not getting back in the water," Madi demanded.

The young responder looked on, confused.

"We'll take her back to the cottage and watch her there," Michael said.

A black, unmarked sheriff's car pulled up. To his surprise

a young woman stepped out of the cruiser in full uniform with her dark hair pulled back in a ponytail.

"You guys okay?" she asked.

"Yes, we are now."

"I've called the doc. He should be here pretty quick."

"We are heading back to our house," Madi said.

The young sheriff pulled out a notepad from her shirt pocket. "What's the address? And I'll have him come by there. With the road knocked out I would feel better if he looked at her."

Madi gave her the address. "Oh, yes, down the street from Webster," the sheriff replied.

"Lenny, can you drive?" Michael asked.

"Yes, sir." She hopped behind the steering wheel and once everyone was loaded, she took off with the sheriff following.

"Are you okay?" he asked Madi.

"Yes, just fuzzy."

After parking, the sheriff came over and started to help with Ally.

"Help her too. She had a close call herself." Michael pointed at Madi.

"I'm fine," she insisted.

Another golf cart with wooden panels on the side pulled in, and a man with gray hair, a gray beard, and thick glasses stepped out with an old-fashioned black medical bag.

"This is the doc," the sheriff said. "And I'm Jenny," she added.

They walked inside Madi's cottage and sat Ally, who was still soaking wet, on the couch. She was still confused but aware enough that she was still sobbing.

"Well, hello, Augustus," Doc said.

"You know the devil bird?" Michael asked.

The doc gave him a peculiar look. "Devil bird? Why, old Augustus is the friendliest bird on the island."

Michael's self-esteem hit rock bottom, *If that's the friendliest bird on the island I would hate to meet the rest.*

"Young lady, you look like you'll be okay once you get some dry clothes on," Doc said after examining her.

"She's got a pretty big knot on the back of her head, probably from one of the concrete posts," he added. Madi felt an overwhelming sense of relief rush through her body. "She's probably going to have a headache, so give her some Tylenol. Sheriff, what about our bridge?" he asked.

"National Guard is handling it. Probably bringing one of those metal folding bridges for the time being," Jenny said.

"I'd like to see her tomorrow and then after the storm. Little lady, you must have one heck of guardian angel," Doc said. Madi smiled at that. *Yes, she does!*

Michael knew the storm was supposed to come in the next afternoon. Looking at the sheriff he started to ask a question, but he became perturbed seeing her pet Gus through the bars.

"All right, folks, you've had enough excitement for one evening. Let's let them rest," he said toward Jenny.

"Call if you need us," Jenny said.

Lenny excused herself with the doc and sheriff and headed home—she'd had enough excitement for one day too.

"I need to call my parents," Madi said, but then realized her phone had been in her pocket when she jumped in. Michael handed his to her. "You have a waterproof case?" she said, looking at his phone.

"Yes, I know I'm a geek."

Michael sat down beside Ally. "You gave us a pretty good scare." He smiled.

"I'm sorry," she yawned.

He turned on the TV to find something for her, but the local channel was broadcasting the weather. He listened closely as the weatherman had a sense of urgency in his voice about the latest news. The storm was now expected to be a category one hurricane by the time it reached the mainland. *Great, first hurricane.*

He could hear Madi in the kitchen, crying while talking with her dad. Michael talked with Ally and hoped she wasn't hearing her mom in tears.

"Maybe we should let Gus out?" Ally said. At first it didn't register with him, then he gave her a concerned look. She started to laugh. "I'm kidding," she smiled.

"You better be." He poked the tip of her nose.

"Thank you. I don't know what I would have done without you," Madi said, walking in and wiping her eyes.

"First you probably wouldn't have been on the pier to start," he said.

"You kidding me? We would have trekked to the end of it," she said.

"Just heard on the news that our storm has been upgraded to a category one hurricane," he said with a worried tone.

"That should make things interesting. My dad wants us to make a trip home as soon as the bridge is fixed."

"Okay . . . I'll watch the devil bird," he said.

"No, you're going with us," she insisted.

Michael turned off the TV and they sat in silence for a while. Looking down at the peach bracelet still tied to Ally's wrist, he saw that she had dozed off.

"Should we let her sleep?" he asked.

"Yeah, she'll be okay."

"I'll let you get some rest too." He looked at Madi. She stared back for a brief moment before asking, "Would you stay tonight?"

He looked at the couch and the big cushions. "Yeah, I'll stay."

She lifted Ally off the couch, put some dry clothes on her, and left her in her room.

Walking back in, she headed straight to the kitchen and pulled down two wine glasses. "We might need two bottles after today," she said.

They spent the rest of the evening checking on Ally, moving between the couch and the front porch, and watching the lightning off in the distance.

Chapter 35

Feeling the sensation of being watched, Michael opened his eyes and expected to see Ally. Instead, he found laser beams shooting from Gus's cage. "Did you stay up all night watching me?" he asked.

Michael stretched his arms above him and kicked off the blanket that fell to the tile floor. Hearing someone in the kitchen, he staggered into the bright space where Ally kneeled on the granite countertop and pulled a bowl from the cabinet. "Here, I'll get that," he said.

"Thank you," she said cheerfully, hopping down and carrying her box of cereal to the table.

"You feel okay?" he asked.

"Yeah."

Hearing the conversation, Madi walked in with her hair in a tangled mess, wearing pajamas and a robe.

"You okay?" Michael giggled.

"I will be after coffee," she said.

"Yep, I'll be right back." Slipping into his flip-flops he made his way to his kitchen for his favorite coffee.

Walking back across the street he bumped into the Hentises.

"Is Ally okay?" Mrs. Hentise asked.

"Yes, close call, but everyone is okay."

"Well, you let me know if you need anything. I'm pulling my

boat out of the water this morning but I can always put it back if you guys need to go to the mainland," Mr. Hentise offered.

"Thank you. I believe we have everything, but this will be our first hurricane."

"I suggest you tarp that piano," Mr. Hentise said.

"I have a cover for it," Michael replied.

"I'll be over today with a tarp and bungee cords. That porch will get soaked."

Michael smiled and accepted his help. He wasn't interested in restoring a new piano, and with everything going on the last few days, he hadn't had much time to write.

The wind had kicked up, and the sun was hidden behind grey clouds that seemed to be turning darker by the hour. Michael walked in with the fresh pot of Nicaraguan coffee and was quickly attacked by a rodeo girl with an empty mug. He didn't resist the attack and quickly took note that Madi needed coffee first thing.

And to his joyous surprise Ally released the beast, so his second attack was the green devil bird. Normally Madi would step in and rescue him, but since she was only on her first cup of coffee, she sidestepped and let Michael take the heat.

Finding the front door cracked open, Lady stuck her head in and put her right front paw inside the door. She excused herself by backing back out when she was the commotion. Instead, she sat patiently on the front porch listening to the attack, secretively praying her dog prayers and being thankful it wasn't her in there.

"Ally!" Michael screamed, still holding the hot pot of coffee, doing his best not to spill it.

Ally ran to his rescue, laughing. "He'll get use to you sooner or later," she said, taking the vulture back to its cage.

Madi stepped back in and kissed Michael on the cheek. "Thank you for staying last night. Ha, now we look alike." She smiled and walked back to the kitchen.

Michael looked over at the mirror mounted on the hallway

wall; his hair was in a tangled mess from the attack. *I hate that bird!*

A giant gust of wind shook the cottage with a low rumble, and Ally shot her mom a worried look.

"It's going to be windy, but we are okay." And with those words of assurance Ally went back to eating her cereal.

Madi and Michael both poured another cup and walked out together to the front porch. They sat only for a short moment, discovering it was too windy to be outside. The thunder was getting louder with the first squall of the storm only miles away.

"Do you think we'll be okay?" Madi asked.

"Yes, I just talked to Mr. Hentise and he said if we need anything to ask him. I am going to run to the store real quick and grab a few things," he said.

Lady had made her way into the hallway and sat staring at Madi. "You can stay here." She smiled at the dog. And as if she understood everything Madi said, Lady wobbled into the kitchen and found a spot under the table.

Michael walked out, shaking his head.

As Michael headed back to get his golf cart, Mr. Hentise met him in his drive with a tarp and bungee cords. "We better wrap it up now. This storm is moving in faster than they had predicted," he yelled above the wind.

Michael generously accepted and together they managed to wrap up his baby grand tighter than a Christmas gift.

"You sure play this thing well. How old were you when you first started?" he asked Michael.

"Oh, eight or nine I guess," and he started in on his story about the orphanage and Robin and Doug.

While sitting on the back porch talking about his past, they both noticed Amos wandering around the beach by himself. "I bet the Wellmans don't know he's out. They can't figure how he gets out of their house. Me? I think they're old and forgetful and leave the door open. Help me catch him," he said.

As they stepped out of the back porch the wind kept the

back screen door from closing. Mr. Hentise and Michael ran out on the beach to fetch the little wiener dog, who believed their running was a game. So he joined in by running from them, and the two men chased him in circles until they were brought to their knees out of breath.

Stopping in front of Michael, Amos dared him to continue the pursuit. "You can stay out here!" Michael said. Amos cocked his head sideways, whimpered, and jetted toward Michael's cabin. Just as he reached it the wind blew the screen door open, inviting Amos inside. "Oh, hell no!" Michael hollered, regaining his breath and running to the cottage.

Bursting in the door, Michael scared the little dog. Amos shot toward the hall out of fear, believing the game of chase was over. Michael caught him as he ran back through the living room, and Amos did the only thing he knew to do—he peed all over Michael and everything that was in the way. Michael quickly ran to the back door with peepee dog spraying wildly at random items. Exploding out the back door and reaching the sand, Amos was done.

"Yep, that's why they call him peepee dog. Funny isn't it?" Mr. Hentise said. Michael wasn't smiling. "And good thing we tarped the piano," he added.

Michael looked back inside to see the pee dripping off the tightly wrapped piano. *Why me?*

Chapter 36

It was close to noon before the first squall line hit the outer banks of the island. It delivered a fury of pelting rain, and wind gust well over the predicted speeds. Madi's cottage shook with every blast, and the high-pitched howling made Madi's skin crawl with concern. "Are you sure we're going to be safe?" she whispered to Michael so Ally wouldn't hear.

"Yes, we'll be fine," he said.

A knock at the door surprised them. *Who in the world would be at the door with a hurricane coming?* Madi thought, walking to the door. Opening the door she found the island doctor on the doorstep. "Hello, Doc, kinda stormy to be out making house calls," Madi said. Stepping to the side she invited him in.

"Oh, this is just a storm. No need to let it stop everything." His bucolic demeanor set Madi's mind at some ease. "It's got to be a big storm for me to stop seeing patients. Why, I remember back in '76 a cat-3 came through here and I saw folks from Old Man Johnson's boat." He kept rambling as he made his way to the living room, expecting Ally to be there. He took off his straw hat off and stopped at the cage for a moment. "Hello, Augustus. You two made up yet?" he asked Michael.

"You need to talk to him," Michael said, pointing to Gus.

"Birds have good memories. He was probably harassed by

someone who looks like you," Doc asserted. "But let's look at our patient." He sat down beside Ally with his stethoscope and listened to her breathing. Michael wondered if she even knew he was there, as her eyes were glued to the TV. "Strong lungs and good heart. I suspect she'll get another ninety years out of them." He rolled over to his knees and fought for a brief moment to get himself up. "Oh, yeah. The National Guard has us a temporary bridge going in as we speak." Michael was amazed with people working during this storm. "So we can get out if need be," Doc added.

Michael and Madi walked Doc out. Holding on to the front door, Madi struggled to get outside. "Are you sure you're going to be okay in this?" she asked him.

"Oh, yes, I'll be fine." Not interested in becoming a kite, Madi walked back in and left the two men to battle the wind on the front porch.

"So how do you like living two doors down from Webster?" he asked Michael.

"I guess okay."

"Have you met them out swimming at night?"

"Not swimming. Why?" Michael asked.

"Oh, just wondering." He started to laugh. "Good luck with Augustus," he said, holding his straw hat and walking to his golf cart.

Within an hour after Doc left the storm picked up with gale-force winds, and lightning began popping all around, rattling the windows. Ally jumped at each crack of thunder, and with a large flash outside their cottage followed by an explosion of thunder, the lights went out.

"Mom?" Ally cried.

"It's okay," she comforted her. They cuddled up on the couch, and with the assistance of a flashlight Madi read to her from one of her favorite children's books. Michael sat quietly watching the two; Ally snuggled as close to her mother as she could get, and Gus leaned against the cage, getting as close too.

Another crash of thunder rocked the cottage and made everyone in the room jump; Gus flapped his wings to stay on his perch. At first Michael didn't have any remorse for the bird until he got up and passed the cage. Instead of his normal rushing the bars at Michael, Gus made a somber chirp. Michael stopped and studied the bird. *Are you setting me up, or you that scared?* Michael moved closer to the cage squinting his eyes with doubt; but to his surprise Gus climbed on the door, wanting out. Madi and Ally watched Michael's bravery, which took their minds off the storm for a short moment. *If you attack me, we are going to see if you can fly in a hurricane*, he deviously thought.

Michael opened the cage, jumping back like he had just lit a firecracker, but Gus quickly climbed out and headed for the girls. Like a trained dog Gus climbed over Madi and snuggled in between the girls for shelter; Michael swore he saw a wink and grin from the devil bird. Truce for the two during this hurricane.

Ally started to fade off with one arm tucked under her mother. Her other arm wrapped around the green parrot, whose eyes were closed—feeling the safeness of Ally's heartbeat.

"I'm going to run across the street and check my place," Michael said, putting his shoes on.

"You don't need to get out in this. I'm sure everything is fine," she said.

"I'll be okay. It looks like it's calmed down." Opening the door Michael found a break in the storm, but the light was becoming scarce as day fell into the evening hours.

He walked around his cottage, looking at the surroundings and making his way to the beach. As he glanced out at the gulf he encountered two sights. One he was expecting—the waves crashing ten to fifteen feet farther onto the sandy beach as normal. The other sight he wasn't expecting—Webster standing halfway to the water, wearing only a pair of blue jean cutoffs with his long hair flapping in the wind. He was staring off into the deep, dark, blue storm.

Michael cautiously walked up to him. "What are you looking at?" he asked the old hippie.

"Oh, man, Michael. Didn't see you. It's coming," he replied, pointing out to sea.

"If you're referring to the storm, it's already here."

Webster smiled, and Michael could see that his eyes were clear and free from dilation.

"Everyone thinks this is a small one but they're wrong," he said.

"What makes you sure?" Michael inquired.

"I just know, but don't let me scare you. We're going to be just fine." Looking back at Michael, he said, "Say, you want to come over for a drink?"

"I'll take a rain check. I've got to get back over to Madi's after I check my place."

"Bro, you two make an epic couple. Hang on to that one!" Webster said.

"Thanks." Michael accepted his advice.

After saying good-bye Michael took a few steps and looked over his shoulder at Webster; he was standing back at attention toward the raging gulf. He couldn't help but take the warning seriously—there was something about the half-naked hippie he trusted. He admired his honesty and loyalty to his friends, and most of all to Sunshine. Michael also couldn't help but wonder what all this weather-beaten hippie had experienced in life. The leather skin and long greying hair showed more than age, but someone who had taken in all of life and its values. *Hippies got one thing right that the rest of us have screwed up—peace.*

Chapter 37

The old hippie was right. Throughout the night the cottage shook with winds well above what had been predicted. Madi lay on the air mattress that Ally was sleeping on and talked with Michael, who reclined on the couch. Both kept a cautious eye on the weather.

Finally by early morning the winds let up, and only a light rain fell over the badly beaten island. At daybreak Michael walked out to find his cottage in one piece but his yard covered in debris. Madi poured Ally a bowl of cereal and joined Michael outside. As they made their way to the beach, waves still crashed litter onto the sand.

"This was worse than they said it would be," Madi said. Looking down the beach it appeared that most of the cottages and homes had some damage; looking toward the Hentises' cottage they spotted Webster rummaging through debris behind his place.

"You guys survived," Webster said as they walked up.

"Yeah, how did you know it was going to be worse than they had predicted?" Michael asked.

"Man, when you been around these storms you just know," he said.

Sunshine walked out onto their back deck in a large T-shirt. "Good morning, guys," she said.

Madi wasn't used to being around people who were so free with themselves. "Good morning." She tried not to stare.

"Few days we'll be able to go back in." Sunshine referred to the surf.

Michael could sense Madi's discomfort. "We are heading into town. You guys need anything?" he asked.

"No, Bro, we're good," Webster said.

"She didn't have anything on but that T-shirt," Madi whispered as they walked off.

Michael hadn't noticed it, and looked back over his shoulder, "She did," he said.

Madi looked back to find Sunshine had lost her shirt and was now baring all. She started to say something when Michael interrupted her. "You can go back and join her if you want." He laughed. She pushed him, causing him to sidestep and almost trip over his own two feet.

ꙮ

Moving a few limbs out of his driveway Michael pulled his golf cart out of the garage and across the street to Madi's. She walked out by herself. "Ally's not going?"

"No, she's playing with Gus."

Driving toward the pier and passing the surrounding restaurants including Randy's Bar and Grill, they were in awe of the destruction to many of the homes and small buildings. Michael had to drive around heaps of debris in the streets, and many times drive through yards just to get to the pier. Coming around the corner their mouths fell open. Randy's was missing part of the roof, and the small taco shack across the street lay in ruins in the bay. Power lines littered the streets, and support poles had toppled over to their sides.

A few people were out surveying the damage and picking up what things they could. Stopping a block from the pier Michael could see Randy standing outside his dilapidated structure. "You need some help?" Michael asked.

Randy seemed dazed and didn't hear Michael the first time, so he asked again. "I don't know what you can do. This will probably end my business," Randy said in a somber tone.

"My goodness. These poor people, their businesses are ruined," Madi said, shocked.

They made their way to Deanne's gym to find the second-story balcony lying on the ground. It had taken half the front wall with it.

Climbing through the rubble Michael could hear someone in the back. "Hello?" he yelled.

Deanne walked out of what was left of her office, her eyes red from crying. "Hey, Michael, quite a mess, huh?" she said.

"You okay?" he asked.

"Yeah, for now." She fought back the tears. He left making sure she had his cell phone number for anything.

Just an hour later, a convoy of National Guard trucks began rolling, indicating they had fixed the bridge or had something in place. After the small convoy passed, they proceeded to the store to discover it in one piece; the same group of old men sat out in front. Michael wondered if they weathered the storm on their church pew.

Jenny's patrol car pulled up, and the dark tinted window rolled down. "You guys okay?" she asked.

"Yes, we are fine, but the damage . . ." Madi was still shocked.

"It's bad but fortunate everyone lived. I imagine the power will be off a week or two," she said.

"We have to go home for a short time. Is there anything we can do here?" Madi asked.

"Pray! Many of these people don't have the insurance coverage they should."

"We will," Madi replied.

"I promised Dad I would come home after Ally's accident." She looked at Michael.

"It's okay," he said.

"Are you still coming?" she asked with a concerned voice.

With a comforting smile, he replied, "Yes, I'm still going."

Driving back to their cottage, she asked, "What can we do to help these people?"

"I might have something we can do."

Chapter 38

The temporary military bridge seemed stouter and more sound than the original blacktop bridge. Ally was strapped in the backseat of Michael's Mercedes already watching a DVD; she was enjoying her fantasy fort that Michael had made her in the car before they left. Madi watched as the two of them made tough decisions as to where the pillows and blankets would go.

As they drove, they were continuously wowed at the downed trees. Makeshift huts on the side of the road had been blown to rubble.

"I'm glad we found Lenny. I'm not sure what we would do with Gus," Madi said.

"I'm sure Doc would care for him. Or what about Sunshine?" He laughed.

"I like Sunshine," the little voice in the backseat shouted.

Michael smiled at her through the rearview mirror. "Yep, she's pretty cool. And free." He shot Madi a teasing gesture.

"I'm still not sure about them," Madi mumbled.

"Oh, they're fine. Just old-school hippies."

"I'm sure you're used to being around people like that, but I'm not."

"Oh yeah, we go swimming almost every morning," he laughed.

"I want to go!" the voice shouted from the back.

"No!" Madi ended the conversation that Michael thought was so funny.

Once on the interstate hunger pains began, the group voted unanimously to stop for lunch. Michael had seen a place on his way to the island that advertised throwing rolls, thinking that would be a unique place. Ally agreed.

Pulling in the parking lot Madi recognized the shape and paint scheme of a barn. "Your kinda place." Michael smiled at her.

"Oh ha ha."

Passing through the glass double doors, Ally's eyes widened as she witnessed a couple of rolls in midflight. The restaurant was buzzing with babble from the tables and loud kids. Not the normal quiet-type place Michael was used to.

"Howdy, folks!" a young pigtailed hostess yelled in a strong Southern accent. Michael's eyes widened at her Southern hospitality.

"Three, please," Madi said, taking over.

Walking to their table Michael felt his hair lift up as if a gust of wind suddenly blew by. Noticing a table of people laughing and pointing his direction, he turned to see a waiter with a basket of rolls pointing his finger at him and winking as he pretended to shoot him. Michael wasn't amused at being a target for someone's food, and was second-guessing his decision.

"Where are you folks from?" a chipper waiter asked, setting down their water.

Michael didn't want to admit being from New York City and be the outcast, but Ally took care of that. "We're from Georgia and he's from New York City," she said, pointing to him.

"New York City!" the young kid yelled for everyone to hear. Instantly four or five other waiters and waitress gave a loud "Yee Ha." Another roll came whizzing by as it reached its destination.

"So, I suggest our chicken-fried steak," the waiter said. "I'll give you a minute." And he left.

Madi sensed Michael's nerves were coming undone. "Relax, have fun. You wanted to eat here." He noticed the same young waiter halfway through his backswing and releasing a roll for the target that was just past Michael. Just like a frog would catch a fly, Michael snatched the roll as it passed over the table. The waiter gave him a funny look and the table behind him started to boo.

"Sorry, I was hungry, and I bet they've got another." Looking back at the waiter, "You think you can get it past me?" he challenged the young man.

Accepting the challenge the young waiter shrugged his shoulders and leaned over in a baseball stance that resembled a pitcher. Half the restaurant started drumrolling on their tables, and the young man released the roll. As it flew over Michael's table he reached up with his hand, but the roll made it through to the targeted table. The restaurant exploded into applause for the young man.

"You don't have to be this relaxed," Madi said, a little embarrassed.

"Michael, you're awesome!" Ally exclaimed, clapping with everyone. That was all he needed to hear. "Sorry, you're outvoted." He smiled at Madi.

"Mommy, see if you can catch one!" Ally said.

"Yeah, Mommy!" Michael taunted.

With the challenge Madi proudly raised her hand to another waiter standing at the other side of the restaurant. With a big smile, he reared back and released a line drive toward Madi's small raised hand. Just as the roll reached her she excitedly dove ahead to catch it, but on her way she saw a glass of water leave the table. At first she thought she was seeing things, but when Michael's smile turned into a gasp, she realized where the glass would end up.

"Oh!" She covered her mouth. Ally joined in by covering her mouth too.

Michael could only react to pulling his shorts away from his now-freezing lap. "What is it with you and tables?" He chuckled.

"I don't know, but at least I got the roll."

After their meal and drying off the trio were back on the road—next stop the Hamlin Farm in Georgia. A few hours later, Michael could see a wrought-iron sign hung over the entrance: "The Hamlin Farm."

"There's Bay!" Ally shouted, flying to the front seat out of excitement.

"Good-looking horse," he replied. He admired the pastures with their horses and grazing cattle, and the barns highlighted by a three-rail white fence. Madi had described it well for him. The farmhouse with white painted trim and siding nestled in the green azaleas sat behind a big solid oak with a tire swing; it was something that he had heard about from both Madi and Ally.

As they pulled up, his heart started pounding and his hands began sweating as he witnessed James and Rena walking out onto the front porch. "I'm nervous," he said to Madi.

She gave him a funny look. "Why?"

"It's been a long time since I met parents," he said.

"Oh, relax. And breathe." She kissed him on his cheek.

Chapter 39

Ally dove out of the car and jumped into James's arms. He swung her around, just missing Rena with her dangling feet. Madi waited for Michael to make his way to her side of the car, but he paused at the hatchback to grab their bags.

"We'll come back for those. Come on." She waved him on. They walked together to the bottom of the steps leading up to the wooden porch.

Madi hugged her mother while her father tried to release the eight-year-old monkey that had leashed herself to him. Letting her down he reached out to shake hands with Michael. "Glad to meet you. We've heard a lot about you," James said.

Michael remembered that the last time Madi was here was just after their misunderstanding. He hoped that was not what James had heard about. "It's nice to meet you too," he answered.

Madi wrapped her arms around her father; she felt the strength in his arms tighten around her, assuring her that he had a lot more life in him.

Rena bypassed Michael's invitation for a handshake by going straight in for a welcoming hug. She sensed that it took him off guard, so she eased the awkwardness. "We hug here in the South," she said.

"Well, okay, thank you," he said.

"Y'all come on in. Too hot to stand on the porch," James replied, opening the kitchen door.

Michael had his hand out for the ladies to enter in front of him; he overheard her mother's whisper on his chivalry. The inside of their house was just like Madi had described it: the décor was 1950s farmhouse, not that they had purposely decorated in that manner—it was that they had never undated it. James wasn't one for change, and years earlier when Rena had tried to replace the couch and his chair, they wound up in huge argument. So she replaced her kitchen appliances and life moved on. Michael watched how Rena carried herself in the kitchen. It was obviously her domain, and she loved it.

"Would you like to see the rest of the place?" Madi asked.

"I would," he said, smiling.

James followed them out the door. "Show me your bags," he said.

"Oh, I'll get them," Michael said.

"Nonsense. You guys go see the place and I'll put them outside of your room." He wasn't taking no for an answer.

"We aren't sleeping in the same room?" Michael whispered to Madi.

"Not unless you want to see my daddy's shotgun collection," she laughed.

As she and Michael walked to the barns, Madi had a skip to her walk—a skip that James hadn't seen in a long time. Walking out of the yard she scooped up Michael's hand and locked her fingers around his before he had a chance to react. As she opened the gate leading into the barnyard, she said in a giddy voice, "Okay, I have to tell you we have a goat that likes to fake people out. He'll rear up and act like he's going to head-butt you, but he'll only fall at your feet. And his name is Goat," she added.

They entered the first barn that was filled with empty stalls, and after making their way through the barn to the back gate, Michael understood what she meant by the endless beauty. The pasture behind the barn seemed to roll with hills long before meeting a tree line.

"Y'all come on!" Madi shouted with her hands cupped beside her mouth.

Michael almost jumped out of his skin. "Y'all?" he questioned.

"It's a Southern thing."

Within seconds the small lot behind the barn was filled with a dozen horses prancing and darting back and forth, excited to get to their stalls for supper. One horse kicked toward another.

"Whoa, he doesn't like that other horse," Michael said.

Madi, who leaned over the gate, looked up at him with a grin. "You city boy."

"If you hadn't figured that out by now, you'll know in the next day or so," he said, still watching the horse fend off the others. Madi pointed to each horse, reciting their names and describing some type of history or story with them.

Michael admired her compassion and love toward the animals; he too could see a glimmer in her eye that wasn't there before. She climbed up on the gate and spun on the top rail to face him, as he leaned over his folded arms on the gate. He cut his eyes over at her to steal a glimpse of her smooth and tanned legs under her shorts. Before he could make any move she hopped down and walked up the hall of the barn, talking about growing up in the barns and seeing horses come and go.

She turned her head and glanced over her shoulder at him. *What a tease!* he thought. Catching up to her he grabbed her hands, which she had strategically placed above her waist and on the small of her back. She gripped his hands tightly.

"Thank you for bringing me to your home," he whispered in her ear, teasing her with his breath.

"You're welcome." She barely got the words out before he spun her around and set her on two bales of hay that were stacked against the wall. Her eyes welcomed him to continue, and she pulled him toward her. Nestling against the bale of hay, he placed his hands on both sides of her face.

As their lips locked her hands ran down his back. He was turned on even more with the thought of her playfully groping his butt. Her touch was soft and even teasing as he became lost in their passionate kiss. She began playing and pushing harder on his butt; then without notice, she pinched the living fire out of him. "Holy crap! Ouch!" He stared into her very confused eyes. Then he realized her hands were hanging off his front pockets.

Spinning around he met Goat. Madi didn't understand his sudden outburst until she saw him rubbing his butt. Laughing, she introduced them. "Goat, this is Michael, Michael, this is Goat." The goat just gave Michael a dumbfounded stare as it chewed its cud. Then Goat sneezed on him and walked away.

"Thanks," he said.

"Don't worry about it. That's Goat."

With a good laugh she jumped down off the bale and looked at her phone for the time. "I guess we can feed this barn for Dad."

"Feed?"

"Yep, open all the stall doors and help me give each bucket in the stall a scoop and a half of oats." She handed him a metal scoop. He followed suit, not wanting to ask any questions and look dumber than he already was.

Once each stall had feed and water ready, Madi grabbed Michael by the hand. "Stand with me," she ordered. Standing close to the gate she pulled it open, and the stampede entered the barn. Just as fast as they entered, each horse disappeared into its own stall.

"Amazing," Michael said.

Smiling at his childlike amusement, she said, "Come on. Let's finish with the others and head in for supper."

Walking out of the barn they ran into James, who was feeding the chickens. "I figured she'd show you the horses first," James said.

Michael worried how long he'd been outside the barn. "I skipped Bay and Grey, figured you'd like to say hi." James smiled at Madi.

Chapter 40

Walking into the next barn over, Michael quickly discovered the interior was state-of-the-art, with rubber-matted floors and climate-controlled temperature. "Wow," he said.

"Yeah, it's nice," she said.

Two horses leaned over their stall doors. "This is Grey," she said, pointing to one of them. "And this is Bay." She ran her fingers through his forelock.

"So this is the infamous Bay?" he said. "He's bigger than the others."

"Not by much, but definitely faster."

"This is a nice barn," he said, stepping back and looking around.

"We built it with the thought of training our rodeo horses like professional athletes. Every little thing helps." She played with Bay's bottom lip, and he tossed his head back and forth. She opened the door and let him walk into the hall with them, draping her arm over his neck and looking down at each step he took. "You're losing that limp," she said.

"He's getting better?" Michael asked.

"Looks like it." Madi led Bay back to his stall, leaving the door open while she mixed feed for the two horses and dumped it in separate buckets. "Here. Dump that into Grey's feed bucket." Closing Bay's stall door, she said, "Let's go eat."

Michael pulled the barn door shut and looked toward the house. Ally was swinging in the tire swing, leaning far back and letting her brown hair drag the dirt underneath. "I could imagine growing up here."

"Could you?" Madi asked.

"Yeah, I believe so. Where are these hay fields?" he asked.

Madi pointed past a white fence. "There's one. Dad just cut it, but past it is another that hasn't been cut."

Michael could see off in the distance where the grass became taller through another fence.

"I'll show you in the morning. You want to see if you can catch one of Mom's rolls?" At first Michael wasn't sure if she was joking, but a hidden giggle said she was.

"Mom, I'm going to show Michael his room then we'll be down," Madi said as she walked through the kitchen.

Michael walked up the creaky set of wooden stairs that led to a hallway with bedrooms scattered throughout. He saw his bag outside one of the doors, and upon looking in he found a double bed with a quilt comforter and matching pillowcases. There were two antique dressers, one with a porcelain bowl on top and another with a small mounted mirror. The room smelled old but had a cozy flair to it, with a window tucked into the wall and ceiling with a small windowseat. The wooden floors creaked and cracked as he walked across them.

"Your dad knew what he was doing by putting me in a room with a motion alarm." He pointed at the floors.

"Just remember, shotguns." She left him standing alone.

Walking down the stairs Michael found everyone already at the table. "I'm sorry, I didn't realize everyone was waiting on me." He felt embarrassed.

"Nonsense, we were catching up with our little girls," James said.

As soon as Michael sat down everyone locked hands. Michael was slow on his reaction, not accustomed to praying over the food and holding hands. After James gave thanks and prayed over the food everyone dug in. "Why do you hold hands when you pray?" Michael asked as an icebreaker.

They all looked at each other for a moment. "Well, I don't know," Rena said. "My family did and we just never stopped." She smiled at Michael.

Changing the conversation, James asked, "So Madi tells us you play the piano and make records." It hit Michael—James and Rena were just as clueless about him as he was about them.

"Yes, started when I was eight." He looked down at Ally.

"Guess what?" she asked the table.

"You're taking lessons," James said with a big grin. She sheepishly smiled back.

"Would you like to play Sunday morning in church?" Rena asked him.

"Church?" He almost choked on his chicken. Rena caught on that maybe he didn't go to church. "Only if you want to," she said.

"Now Rena, don't go making plans for the boy." James worked on getting him out.

"Maybe so," Michael answered. Rena settled back in her seat.

Changing the subject James said, "After supper I'll show you my shotgun collection." Michael choked.

Madi also choked on a small piece of meat and snorted out of her nose. Michael quickly chugged down some water to relieve his throat, which was in a tension spasm. Madi did all she could to fight back the building explosion of laughter. James looked confused at the choking musician and his daughter snorting food out of her nostrils.

"Did I say something?" James asked.

"No, sir." Michael wiped his mouth with the white cloth napkin in his lap. "I'd like to see your shotgun collection." He kicked Madi under the table.

"That was a great meal, Mrs. Hamlin," Michael said.

"Please call me Rena, and thank you," she said.

"Come on, Michael. Let's get out of the way while the girls clear the table," James said.

Michael looked back at Madi. "It's okay, go!" she said, waving him off with her hand.

James and Michael walked out onto the wraparound porch and sat in a couple of rocking chairs. "This is really a nice place you have here," he said.

"Well, thank you. It's been in the family for quite some time. It's hard work but it has its rewards."

The sun was starting to set over the rolling pasture behind the barns. Michael didn't say anything, hoping Madi would quickly join them; he didn't want her to miss it.

"Girls, get out here!" James yelled. The three generations of girls walked out in time to watch the sun set beyond the fields, causing the sky to explode into an orange backdrop. Nobody said a word; the reflection of the colors bouncing off the hay fields mesmerized everyone by the beauty that was created.

Rena disappeared back inside as Madi and Ally took to the white wicker swing hanging from the ceiling. As the evening quickly set in and the fields turned dark, the lightning show began and fireflies engulfed the yard. Ally ran inside and returned with a glass jar and an ice cream cone.

"Hey, half-pint! Where's ours?" James sat up.

"It's coming," she said, jumping off the last two steps onto the ground. Rena walked out carrying a tray of four ice cream cones that had already begun to melt. "I hope you like ice cream," she said to Michael.

"Oh yes, maybe too much." They devoured their desserts as they all watched Ally chase fireflies.

"So has my little girl played for you yet?" James asked.

"Dad!" Madi tried to quiet him.

"Played?" Michael looked at Madi while he took the last bite of his cone.

"The violin?" he asked.

Now Michael was dumbfounded. "You play the violin? You said you didn't have any music ability."

"Well, I said I didn't play the piano," she replied.

James got up and disappeared inside, and before the screen door had shut he was back out with a black case. "Here, play something," James demanded.

"Dad, not now."

"I would have to agree with Dad. Play something," Michael said.

She gave him a funny look. "Unless you can't," he said. He had learned how to push her buttons. Her funny look changed to squinted eyes, and she accepted the challenge—something he was getting used to seeing.

She opened the fur-lined case and pulled out a beautiful dark violin and bow; she placed it under her chin and checked the tuning. Michael sat back in his chair, intrigued with this hidden talent. *Can she play?*

The evening air filled with the sounds of Mozart as Michael watched her go through the motions of every note. She sat up with her shoulder pushed forward and her head holding the instrument. She rocked with every tempo change, and with eyes closed felt her way through the piece that changed history. Once finished she lowered the dark marbled wooden instrument and looked at Michael for approval. He sat hypnotized at talent and beauty. "Wow!" was all he could get out.

"Mommy, that was nice," Ally said, passing by and chasing a firefly.

"Okay, now you know and now I'm embarrassed," she said.

"For what? That was beautiful!" he said. She smiled and closed the case.

"Ally looks like she needs help," she said, joining her daughter.

"I know I shouldn't say this because it might scare you, but we are so happy you're here. We haven't seen our baby girl laugh or smile for two years. Thank you." Rena leaned over and kissed Michael on the cheek.

Normally he would have melted in his seat out of embarrassment or have been scared off like Rena said. But watching Madi chase the fireflies and seeing her looking back at him laughing with Ally, he was dug in . . . in love.

Chapter 41

Michael opened his eyes to find Ally standing beside his bed, staring at him.

"Oh good, you're awake," she said.

"I am now. What's up?"

"Breakfast, silly." She grinned.

He then heard a voice from down the hall: "Ally, you better not be waking up Michael," Madi said.

Sticking his head around the corner of Madi's room, he said, "Too late."

"I'm going to strangle her." Madi was sitting on the bed, still in her nightshirt and thumbing through some pictures. She slid off the bed on the opposite side and slipped into her shorts.

"You hungry?" She smiled.

"I am."

She looked down the hall, and seeing Ally had disappeared downstairs, she grabbed his shirt and pulled him down to her level, almost pulling him off his feet and kissing him on the lips. "Good morning," she replied in a soft warm tone.

He pushed his way into the bedroom. "It could be a really good morning."

She put her hand on his chest stopping him and then raised her index finger. "Shotguns!" She smiled. He laughed and followed her down the stairs, briefly holding hands till they reached the bottom.

"Remember me saying I might have an idea to help everyone on the island?" he asked, walking into the kitchen.

"Yes." Madi searched for coffee cups.

"I want to put on a benefit concert and call in a few favors from some other artists."

Her eyes lit up. "Michael, that's a great idea. People would come from all over."

"And I had a vision of someone playing with me on a song or two."

"Who?" she asked, watching the coffee pour from the pot to the cup.

"You!"

Coffee splashed out of the cup and onto the countertop and down the cabinet. "Me! I don't think so."

"Are you kidding me? You played better last night than many concert violinists."

She placed his cup in front of him. "Drink your coffee and quit dreaming."

Her dad folded down his paper and faced her. "Chicken!" he said.

"Cluck cluck," she replied.

"Stay on her," James told Michael.

Rena sat a huge plate of pancakes, bacon, eggs, and hash browns in front of Michael. He looked down at the plate at the heaping amount of food and began sweating; he wasn't sure what to say or do. He looked up and smiled at Rena. "Thank you," he squeaked out.

She started laughing. "I'm teasing you. Madi said you have a strict diet."

She moved the plate toward James.

Madi set down a plate of dry toast and fruit for him. *Whew, that was close,* he thought.

City boys! James thought.

"Well, I know you two had plans this morning," James started with a mouthful of pancakes, "but rain is moving in this afternoon, and the hands that were coming to help with working the cattle can't make it this morning. I could use you two."

Madi jumped in defense of Michael. "Dad, I'm not sure that we—"

Michael interrupted her. "We'd be glad to help," he said, secretly trying to earn points from the country folks who were feeding him.

"You ever rode a horse?" James asked him.

Michael's heart started beating faster. He had just been interested in helping, and now he was getting himself into something he would have a hard time faking. "To be honest, no." He felt stupid. Madi was a little shocked. Out of all the talking they had done about her horses and farm, she'd never asked him that question. He had just listened.

James just stared at him across the table, and now Michael was really feeling dumb. But what he didn't know was that James was admiring his honesty. *Most boys or men would lie about that to impress the girl, but this young man would rather impress me by telling the truth.* What James didn't know is that Michael didn't want to lie about riding, knowing he would look worse falling off a horse in front of Madi.

"Well, we will teach you. Actually it's pretty easy. I'll give you my horse," he said. Madi smirked and looked at her dad. *His favorite horse that he won't let anyone ride.*

"Slow down, Ally. You're going to choke yourself," she said, watching Ally stuff her face. The kitchen air filled with laughter and enjoyment as the five of them ate breakfast and listened to Michael tell stories of shark fishing and about Webster. Madi had scooted her chair closer to him and kept a hand on his back and shoulder. Rena placed her hand on James's knee for his attention, and when Michael and Madi were looking away she smiled at James and nodded toward the couple.

"I really want to call Jenny and ask her about the concert. Do you mind?" he asked Madi.

"No, go call her. Leave me out of this."

On the front porch he talked with Jenny, who fell in love with the idea. "I want to talk to the mayor about this. I know he'll love it."

Michael said, "Who is the mayor?"

There was a short pause on the line. "Doc. You didn't know that?"

"Ha! No, I didn't. Small world."

They set the date: three weeks from that Saturday.

As Michael returned to the kitchen, James said, "Bad news."

"What?" Michael asked.

"Some of the boys already put up the cattle this morning, so no riding horses today. You guys can go do what you had planned."

Michael could almost hear the hint of disappointment in his voice. "We'll still help," he said.

James perked up and didn't turn his offer down. "Great. Let's get ready."

Madi started to say something but her dad shut her down. "Nope! Y'all are helping," he said.

Pulling up to the cattle pen Michael was still admiring the one-ton dually, thinking it was the biggest truck he had ever ridden in. Hopping out he helped Ally climb down from the back of the truck, then he followed James and Madi up to a group of other men. All of them had on blue jeans, boots, and some kind of button-down, long-sleeved shirt; a few of them wore cowboy hats. He wondered why someone would wear long sleeves in this kind of heat, when one of the men wearing a cowboy hat picked up Madi and twirled her around as though she was a little girl. With a big smile she introduced him. "Michael this is Pat. He was one of Cole's best friends."

Instantly he felt funny; here he was the new boyfriend, and he wasn't sure how they would accept him. Pat reached out for his hand. “Hey, Michael. Any friend of Madi’s is a friend of ours,” he greeted him. *Ours?* It now dawned on him that all these men were friends of Cole and the Hamlin family. He felt uncomfortable.

“Let’s get busy before it rains,” James said. Each man seemed to know his role, leaving Michael unsure where he belonged. “Michael, you help me,” James said.

James handed Michael a fiberglass stick with a black handle on it. “Here—you’ll need this.” Michael just stared at the tall, thin, yellow pole. “Don’t worry. I’ll tell you what to do. They are going to let twelve to fourteen pairs in, then we are going to separate the cows from the calves.”

Sounds easy, he thought.

Wrong.

Pat opened a silver gate and twelve pairs ran in. Michael knew he was supposed to push the cows to James and the calves to another guy, but that wasn’t working.

“Use that pole!” James hollered. Michael was too busy leaping over cow patties, and every time he did, the pair would run the other way.

“You’re going to have to forget about stepping in crap. It’s going to happen,” Pat yelled, pointing at his manure-smeared boot.

Finally he turned one cow toward James and the calf toward Pat. “Yeah, that’s it, City!” Pat yelled. That built his confidence, and he turned pro cowboy for a short time. After everything was separated they started running the cows through the chute for shots and fly tags. Michael found himself pushing cattle the rest of the morning.

Rain set in shortly after, settling the dust that had stirred up while they released the cattle back into the pasture. “Hey! Shorty, you and City meet us at the Silver Buckle tonight!” Pat hollered at Madi.

“Shorty?” Michael asked.

“Pat has the tendency to nickname everyone,” she answered.

"So I gathered, City?"

"He doesn't mean any harm by it."

James slid in the driver's seat and cranked the diesel engine. "Y'all ready?" he said, not waiting for an answer beforc pulling out.

Once they returned to the farm Michael was ready to wash his hands. Afterward they lounged around the house with rain pounding outside.

"I guess it's too wet to walk out to the fields?" he said.

"Yeah, it will be dry for tomorrow," she said.

"You want to go to the Silver Buckle tonight?"

"Nah, you might not like it," she said.

"I don't mind. You need to go see your friends. When was the last time?"

"It's been awhile. I would like to go."

"Then we'll go," he finished.

Chapter 42

Meeting Madi downstairs, Michael had on shorts and a short-sleeved button-down shirt. "I wore the only blue jeans I had today," he said.

"You're fine. Dad, we're taking the truck," she hollered to the kitchen. "You behave and be in bed by ten." She kissed Ally on the forehead.

Walking to the truck Michael held his hand out and Madi grabbed it.

"No, keys! I'm not letting you drive me to a bar," he said.

"It's a bar and grill," she sassed, handing him the keys with a smile. "Are you sure you can drive a truck?"

"We're going to find out."

Pulling up he found a parking space out front that didn't require any maneuvering. "See? Nothing to it," he said.

"Yep, you did good," she said. *I hope dad doesn't get a ticket for us parking in a handicap spot.*

The inside was a pleasant surprise to Michael; there were many families with kids throughout the restaurant. He had in his mind that they were going to a hick bar with pool tables, dartboards, and smoky air. In the back sat a group of high tables with bar stools surrounding them, holding the young men who had helped with the cattle earlier that day.

Pat spotted them walking in. "Shorty!" he yelled and waved

them back. It seemed that most of the crowd was couples with either their girlfriends or wives scattered throughout. Madi hugged Pat's wife while the other women waited their turn to welcome Madi with a hug.

"You play pool, City?" Pat asked.

Michael noticed the tables set around the corner. "I wondered if there would be any in here."

"Hell, son, this is a bar and grill." Pat smirked.

"Not now, Pat. Let us get something first," Madi told him.

The waitress walked up. "Madi Coverton! Don't you look awesome. If I didn't like men I'd be after you," she said. "And I assume this is the man." She grabbed Michael's hand.

Madi turned red. "This is Michael."

"What do y'all want to drink, sweetie?" she asked.

"Two beers, and do you still have that shrimp platter thing?" Madi asked.

"You betcha!"

Throughout the night they laughed at old stories about Madi. Some included Cole but most were about her rodeos and high school. Michael wondered if they kept the Cole stories down on account of him.

"Thank you for putting up with my mother's cooking. You know us in the South—we're going to fry it," she said.

"It's okay, these shrimp are good," he replied.

"Do you play pool?" he asked her.

Cocking her head, she said, "Yes, do you?" Before she could get an answer he turned to Pat. "I've got my partner. You?" Michael said, pointing to an empty pool table.

"Hell yeah, City." Pat grabbed his wife, who was in the middle of a conversation.

"Pat, I was talking."

"Come on, woman. City and Shorty have challenged us."

Pat broke the racked set of pool balls and made a couple of shots. Madi stepped up and missed her first. After Pat's wife made her first three shots, Pat said, "City, you might have walked into the wrong game!"

Madi became nervous, but her lack of confidence in Michael quickly vanished when he ran the table to the last shot on the eight ball. "Damn, Madi, you didn't tell us you brought a pool shark."

Pat was impressed and Michael was quickly gaining respect, but he missed the eight ball. Pat pounced on the opportunity and sank all his shots, including the eight ball. But Michael had proved himself on the table. The next five games bounced back and forth between Pat and Michael as the girls watched on with everyone else.

"Good games!" Pat gave Michael a high five. "Now, Madi tells us you're a piano player." He walked over to a keyboard that was covered by a black cloth. "Would you?" he asked.

Madi stepped in. "You don't have to."

"Nah, I don't mind." He turned to Pat. "What do you want to hear?"

"Hell, something we can two-step to." Michael had lost the nickname *City* for now, but Madi was worried that it was about to quickly return. *Does he even know what two-step is?*

Michael shot her a glance.

"Country," she mouthed.

"What's country?" he teased her.

Making his way around the keyboard, he flipped the switch and the speakers popped. Then to Madi's surprise he pulled up a microphone and tapped the end of it to see if it was on. "Two-step, huh?" he repeated in the microphone. With those words everyone took it as an invitation, and as they moved a few empty tables the dance floor was set. He quickly programmed the keyboard with a beat, and he joined in with the keys; and before they knew it, Michael was playing a popular country song. Just a few measures into the piece, he added the words and sang the first country song he had sung in many years. Madi was coming to the realization that there was nothing he couldn't do with a keyboard.

She sat at a table sipping on the longneck bottle, watching Michael entertain her old friends. She thought back to how many times she and Cole had been there on the weekend with this same group of people. Their love and support through his coma and death meant so much to her, but now accepting her friend showed their true loyalty to her. They too sensed her happiness. Tears built up in her green eyes as she realized that she was happy—something she had missed for a long time.

Getting up from her stool she made her way across the dance floor as Michael sang with a smile aimed at her. Sliding a chair over she joined him at the keyboard. One place that Michael felt at home and had mastered was behind a set of keys. He finished the upbeat country song and pulled the microphone closer to his mouth.

"You guys want to speed things up a bit?" A big roar came from the dance floor, and a young guy pulled up a bar stool close to the keyboard and sat a guitar in his lap.

"You play and I'll follow," the young guy told Michael. They played through the following song, and then another young guy sat behind the set of drums and joined in. Before Michael realized it there was a full band playing.

Michael, thinking it was the perfect end to a messed-up day, got one more surprise when Pat made his way over to him.

"You better dance with this girl before she finds someone else."

He helped Madi out of her seat. Then Pat sat down behind the keyboard. "You'll have to give me some pointers after," he said, and Pat played into the next slow song.

Michael and Madi joined the others on the dance floor, and he rested his hands on her waist. She flipped her hair back and gazed into his eyes. "Bet you never thought you'd be in a country bar on a dance floor with me," she said.

"Madi, you are one beautiful woman. I don't know any other place I'd rather be." Then he kissed her.

Chapter 43

Michael opened his eyes once again to the steady glare of an eight-year-old; she had her chin propped up on the side of the bed. "You up?" She stood up with excitement.

"Yep. So what is for breakfast?" He smiled, trying to hide his morning breath.

"I'm having waffles. Mom is fixing you something that looks like oatmeal but smells funny."

"Why don't you go tell your mom she can have that yucky stuff. I'm eating waffles with you," he said.

"Okay! Grandma always has the best maple syrup." She disappeared out the door. Michael could hear her running down the wooden stairs and Madi asking her if she had been in his room.

"Can we go ride this morning?" Ally asked Madi.

Madi looked at Michael for a read. He smiled back. "I guess so." She poked Ally on the nose with her spoon. James was missing from the table because his day always started early this time of year. Michael crammed the last bite of waffle in his mouth, the maple syrup making it dissolve in midbite.

"Are you done?" Rena said, looking at his empty plate.

"Wow, those were really good. Thank you," he replied, wiping his mouth.

"Dear, I got this. You and Michael go drink your coffee," Rena said as she took a plate from Madi.

The two of them walked out on the front porch. Madi cuddled up in a rocking chair while Michael sat on the railing that wrapped around the porch. The sun was just peeking over the barns, and the warmth of the Georgia morning felt fresh after a long day of rain.

Michael could see a tractor in the farthest field. "What is your dad doing?"

Madi craned over the railing to see. "Raking hay. It's what he does." She settled back in her chair.

"Where do you see yourself in the future? I mean, are you planning to stay here?" he asked.

"I don't know, I haven't given it much thought. This is home and I feel safe here. But . . . I don't know. What about you?"

"I never really had a home. I mean, New York is kind of home. But I have nothing tying me down there. I guess I'll see where life takes me." He sipped his coffee.

Michael watched as James got out of his cab-tractor and opened a gate. He wondered how many times James had been through that gate. Madi secretly watched Michael. The warm morning breeze caught his hair, flipping it up, and she stared at his eyes as they scanned the surroundings to take it all in.

He felt the gaze from Madi, who was still trying to be stealthy. "What do you see?" he asked.

The question threw her off, and she figured she was busted. "The future," she softly said with her lips on the side of her cup.

A little head peeked around an open door. "Mommy, you said we could go riding." Madi wasn't sure if Ally's timing was bad or good.

"Go get your boots." She smiled at her. The door slammed and the sound of footsteps ran wildly through the house. "Well, are you ready?" she asked Michael.

"For the future," he slyly said.

Once at the barn, Madi pulled the barn door open and led

three horses into the hall. Ally forcefully grabbed one of the lead ropes and tied her horse to a stall. She didn't want any help from her mom; she was more interested in showing Michael that she could saddle her own horse.

Once everyone was saddled, Madi showed Michael some pointers then climbed on. Michael didn't have any trouble. They rode through a few of the cut hay fields and toward the tree line. "There is a great creek back here," Madi said, turning back to Michael. He was still focusing on his balance, but he wasn't going to let his rookie status get in the way of keeping up with the girls.

They rode the tree line for a ways, then found an opening leading down toward the creek. The opening was well-worn and obviously the main way. The creek was running high with the previous day's rain, and Ally didn't hesitate walking through the water and into the middle.

Michael found that the deepest part of the creek was belly deep to the horses, and as he watched Madi fold her legs over the saddle horn to stay dry, he figured he better just raise his shoes.

After riding for over an hour they came back out of the tree line and into a pasture. James was raking in the field nearby. They stopped and watched him finish his last few laps around the field, and pulling his tractor close to the field he shut it off. "You three lost?" He smiled.

"We rode through the creek and Michael didn't fall off," Ally shouted over the fence.

James had the expression of someone being busted; Michael wondered if James thought he would fall off.

"That sounds like fun. I have to go to the feed store. Half-pint, why don't you go with me?" he asked Ally.

She turned to Madi. "Can I?"

"Yes, but wash off before you leave," Madi replied.

"You kids have fun," James said, shutting the door and

firing up the tractor. Madi wondered if he was just giving them some alone time.

They watched as Ally led her horse and opened and shut the gates for James as they headed back to the barn.

"You want to see one of the uncut fields?" Madi asked.

"I thought you weren't going to ask."

They passed the cut field James had just finished—the grass laid in rows with a sweet smell in the air. Soon Michael found himself in a thick field of grass that was waist-high, and he and Madi climbed down and led the horses for a bit. Madi slipped the bridles off the horses and let them graze as they found a spot. As if on cue the wind picked up and the tips of the blades folded in different directions. The sun beamed down and turned the grass a tint of blue with the wind in one direction, and then a hint of purple with another direction.

"I see what you've been talking about; the grass seems to change colors," he said.

"It changes all during the day, and at sunset you can lie here and watch the sun setting over the fields. It looks like the sun is going to set it on fire," she replied. A gust of wind blew past them toward the barns and Madi reached out and took his hand, her anchor bracelet falling against his wrist. She sat down, pulling his arm downward to join her. Expecting the ground to be wet he was astonished to find the ground dry. Taking cue from Madi he lay back with his arms folded behind his head; the clouds seemed to pop out at them as they passed by. He thought for a moment and realized he hadn't paid them much attention while riding.

"I have spent so much time out here, it seems to be the only place I can clear my head," she said.

He lay, still listening to her voice and the sound of the wind as it cut through the tall grass. *This is somewhere I could easily get used to,* he thought. He felt her hand cross over his chest and her leg wrap around his. Turning his head he found himself inches from her face. They just stared at each other for what seemed like hours; the horses grazed up to them and then wandered on past. They were completely hidden, sunk in the sea of Bermuda with only the two horses knowing where they were.

Michael started to say something but was interrupted by Madi's kiss; she placed her hand on the side of his face and twirled his hair with her fingertips. She repositioned herself by sliding on top of him. Her hair fell on both sides of his face, concealing their kiss. He wrapped his arms around her waist and entwined his fingers, locking her in.

Feeling something moist on his cheek he tried to ignore it, but it only seemed to expand. Pulling away, he saw the tears in her eyes. "What's wrong?" he asked.

She could feel the warmth from his breath. "Nothing, I'm okay," she tried to continue.

"No, something is wrong," he persisted.

With her hair still draping over her face, she said, "They're good tears." She fought back the words she really wanted to say: *I love you.*

Chapter 44

The ride back to the barn wasn't what Madi had in mind. She didn't want the day to end, and she was dying to know what Michael was thinking. Had she let too much of her guard down? Was she scaring him off? She wasn't sure how to act, having only fallen in love twice in her life. Once with Cole, and now.

Michael pulled his phone out while helping Madi unsaddle. "Jenny just texted me to let us know the power is back, and they want to talk about the concert."

"Go call her, I got this," Madi said.

"Nah, I'll call in a minute." He persisted in helping.

"Michael, I grew up doing this. Go call." Without arguing he stepped out of the barn with his phone glued to his ear.

Madi finished putting up the saddles and led the horses to a rack for washing. "Grey," she began, talking to both horses, "I can't believe I feel this way toward him. Do I have time for a relationship? Would he have time? We both have lives on the road and I'm not sure who travels the most. I am falling in love with him!" She continued babbling to both horses, not knowing Michael had walked up. At first he thought she was singing, then he heard his name and eavesdropped from around the corner. As he tuned in to her rambling on about him, he began to feel guilty as if he were reading her diary. He put the phone up to his ear and yelled, “Okay, thanks, we’ll be in touch.” He rounded the corner to warn her that he was there.

She turned her head and smiled. “Everything okay?”

“Yep, getting organized.”

She watched him push his phone in his front pocket, then she squirted him with the hose. “Oops, sorry.”

He gave her a funny look, not sure if that was on purpose. “I should probably head back to the island first thing in the morning. Robin and a few promoters are flying down tomorrow to start the organization of the concert. We already have a few other recording artists that want to help,” he said.

“That’s great. We can leave tomorrow. Honestly, I’m ready to get back.”

ꟹ

The next morning Madi was loading the last bag into the hatchback of Michael’s Mercedes. “We’ll be back in less than five weeks. It’s hard to believe that this summer is almost over,” she said to her dad, who leaned on the open hatch.

“What are your plans after?” he asked.

“Well, Bay is ready now and with another five weeks of rest—”

“That’s not the plans I meant,” he interrupted.

“I don’t know, Dad. Maybe we’ll plan to see each other. We haven’t talked about it,” she answered, knowing exactly what plans he was insinuating.

Michael walked out onto the front porch with Rena. “Thank you again for your hospitality.” He was carrying a bag of snacks she had prepared for them on the road.

After hugging her he walked down the wooden steps where James was waiting for him. “Take care of my girls,” James said, holding out his hand.

“Yes, sir, I will.”

Ally rolled down her window from the backseat, where she had already gotten comfortable. "Bye!" she yelled out.

Both James and Rena walked up to the back window to say their good-byes. They stood arm in arm and watched the black Mercedes disappear in a cloud of white dust.

"Are we stopping at the roll-throwing place?" Ally asked, as they got on the interstate.

"We've already eaten, sweetheart. There are snacks here." She gave her the bag Rena had sent with Michael.

With three movies and midmorning traffic, their drive back was quicker and quieter than Michael had expected. "Well, I guess I got out of playing for your parents' church," he said, striking up conversation.

Madi, who had been glued to a book, looked out of the corner of her eyes. "Trust me, you didn't get out of that."

Michael looked down at the book she was reading. "*Waterproof*? Is it any good?"

"Yes." She held it up to show him the cover.

The closer to the island they got the more trees they noticed uprooted from the powerful winds. It was a clear day, and the temperature had rapidly climbed the farther south they got.

Ally rolled down her window and stuck her head out. "I can smell the salt water already," she said.

"Ally, roll up your window," Madi fussed at her.

"Oh, she's okay. It's not bothering me," he said.

Crossing the temporary bridge leading onto the island, they saw just as much destruction as they did before they left; but the island buzzed with volunteers helping to pick up debris. Trees that had been cut to allow passage throughout the roads lay in fresh sawdust, with piles of roofing materials and insulation thrown along the ditches. Deanne's gym hadn't been touched, and the second-story porch still blocked the entrance. She was standing outside looking at her building.

Pulling over and stepping out, Michael asked her, "You doing okay?"

"I don't know. The insurance people have come by and now I have to get someone in here to remove everything to start rebuilding." Her voice was shaky.

"Can we buy you lunch?" Michael asked, seeing the pizza place was open across the street.

"Nah, I'm good," she answered.

Ally broke from her movie once she heard the word *pizza*. "Mom, I'm hungry."

"If you want to run by the cottage we can order," he said.

"I'm hungry, too," Madi said. "And we would love for you to join us, "she said to Deanne.

"Okay," Deanne agreed.

Unknown to Deanne, Michael had already planned his next few mornings and they included clearing the debris from the gym.

The aroma of fresh baked bread and tomato sauce flooded the air and stirred their hungry stomachs. The old wooden floors creaked as they made their way across to a booth. Ally and Deanne slid in on one side. Deanne was young, ambitious, and a fighter; Michael had a strong sense that she wasn't going to let a hurricane shake her business.

"If I get some guys together would you let us clear that debris from your building?" he asked.

She looked wide-eyed at Michael's questions. "I take that as a yes," he said.

"Normally I'm not much on aid, but I . . ."

"We insist. Plus it gives me a chance to give back to the islanders," Madi interrupted.

A big smile formed across her once depressed face. "I'll definitely train you guys at no charge."

"Nope! Consider it part of our training," Michael said.

Before she could rebut, a young waiter joined them. "What are y'all drinking?" he asked. "Hi, Deanne," he added sheepishly. At saying hello Deanne smiled and turned a light hint of red. Madi grabbed Michael's leg, hinting there was love in the air.

Ally asked Deanne a million questions—from where she was during the hurricane, to her favorite color. Deanne started her story of finishing school in Pennsylvania and being madly in love with another grad student. They had plans of marrying and moving to New York, but finding him with another woman abruptly ended their relationship and devastated her with the pain of a broken heart. She had moved to the island to clear her head and had fallen in love with the people and the area.

The young waiter sat down their pizza, ending the story.

Chapter 45

Walking in Madi's cottage they were greeted by an excited green parrot that demanded to be let out of his cage, although Michael questioned the decision. Leaving the front door open while bringing in their bags, Lady waddled in with her tongue hanging out and teeth showing. "My, all the animals are glad to see us," Madi said, bending over and petting the basset hound.

After getting Madi and Ally situated, he started to his cottage. Ally stopped him with a flyer she had picked up from the pizza place. "You said you would take me." She showed him. It was a rental place with scooters, kayaks, surfboards, and stand-up paddleboards.

"Yes I did, and you, my beautiful young lady, are fearless. Much like someone else I know," he said. A large grin formed across Madi's face as she overheard from the kitchen.

"Heading to my place," he yelled.

"Here, I'll walk with you. Ally, watch Gus," she said.

Michael backed his Mercedes across the street without turning around.

"It feels good to be back," she said.

"Bring that bag with you." He chuckled.

It seems I've been here and done this before. Wonder if it will turn out the same way. She grinned inside. He unlocked the front door and held it open for her to drag a bag through. When she set it down and turned to face him, he swept her up in his arms and planted a big kiss on her. *Yep, same way!*

She wrapped her legs around him once again, and he carried her to the couch. Gently placing her on the couch he positioned himself on top of her. Their kiss became hotter and more intense; he felt her hands under his shirt and on his back. Then right on cue, he felt the sensation of luring eyes; without unlocking lips he struggled to search the floor for Lady but she wasn't in sight. Then he felt the clawing on his back becoming forceful and violent. With a sudden pierce of his skin, he yelled, "Ouch!" He looked at the puzzled look on Madi's face, when he felt another pierce. He shot up and grabbed his back, and green feathers littered the couch. *You've got to be freaking kidding me!*

Gus fell to the floor. "What the!? How did he get in here?" Michael exclaimed. Normally Gus's attacks were somewhat funny, but Madi was puzzled at how he got in the cottage too. She raised up and looked over the floral couch toward her house, where through Michael's open door she saw her front door open and Ally wandering the front yard looking up.

"I swear this devil bird is out to kill me," he said, holding his back.

She quickly scooped up the parrot and headed toward the door. "I'll be right back," she said, storming off. As she walked across the front yard he could hear her talking with Ally and correcting her about leaving the front door open. He found bandages in the bathroom and wrestled to apply them to the fresh bite marks on his back. *Surfboards would be much safer.*

Once settled Madi and Michael made their way out to the beach. The waves seemed almost nonexistent and the water a clear, emerald green. "It's hard to believe that something can be so violent and within a day be so beautiful and calm," she said. The words stuck with Michael.

"Welcome back," a voice said from behind them. Turning they found the Hentises and Wellmans.

"Hello, how are you guys doing?" Michael asked.

"You kids didn't run off and get married, did you?" Mrs. Hentise questioned.

"Don't ask that. You're putting Michael on the spot!" Mr. Hentise snapped.

"No, Mrs. Hentise, we didn't get married." Madi smiled.

"Let us know if you kids need anything. Food is just now getting back to the island," Mr. Hentise said.

"Thank you. Oh, and Mrs. Hentise, you inspired me to have a concert here. We are planning a benefit concert in the next few weeks," Michael said.

She elbowed her husband. "Told you he'd play here."

Madi and Michael sat in the white sugar sand watching the sunset. "It seems like it's setting slower," he said.

Placing her head on his shoulder and snuggling closer, she whispered, "Good."

They sat in silence watching the sun disappear into the sea. "It's unique. In the fields it looks like the sun in setting them on fire, but here it looks like the ocean is putting out the sun," he said. She just sat and listened to the vibrations of his voice radiating through his chest.

He pulled her up to her feet, and she wanted to resist but knew they needed to check on Ally. "I have a bottle of red," he said.

"You know, tonight just seems like a beer night." She smirked.

"Do you think we could surf tomorrow?" he asked.

"You're going to laugh at me, but I have no balance when it comes to boards."

"You ride horses!"

"Ride! Not stand," she answered.

"You can try." He wasn't taking no for an answer.

That evening they sat on the front porch of her cottage

talking about the concert, the farm, and why Gus hated him so much. “I hope you don’t mind, but I’m going to turn in early,” she said. As he stood he went to peck her on the lips, but she quickly jumped up on a small table and threw her arms around him, locking her lips to his. After a moment she said, “Thank you for going to meet my family,” face-to-face with him.

“I hope I get to spend more time with them,” he said.

The warmth of new love shot up Madi’s spine. *Me too!*

As she lay in bed running her fingers through Ally’s hair, Madi reflected back to vision she had of Cole in the field. From their conversation, she knew with all her heart he was happy and at peace for her. She thought for a second she heard something, and as she lay still and concentrated, she heard the faint sound again. Then, like magic, the notes floated in her open window, filling her bedroom with a beautiful melody from across the street. She rolled over on her back and placed her arms above her head. Fixated on the music she breathed with every change in tempo. *Michael, I love you!*

Chapter 46

A light knock on the door made Madi look up from her morning coffee, and another knock sounded before she could open the door. Michael wore an astute grin, along with board shorts, white tank top, visor, and flip-flops. "You girls ready?" he asked.

"For?" Madi asked.

"Paddleboarding!" he excitedly answered. "Since there aren't any waves, surfing was out. So, stand-up paddleboards."

"I am going to have to finish my coffee. You're too energetic in the morning," Madi said.

Following her in he was grateful to find Gus locked in his cage. Gus lunged forward as if striking at Michael when he walked past the cage. "Where's Ally?" he asked upon finding the kitchen empty.

"Lenny stopped by and they headed to the beach." Madi was still in pajama bottoms and an oversize long-sleeved shirt. "That was beautiful last night," she said, referring to his playing.

"Thank you. I believe I am close to finishing what I set out to do."

"What's next?"

"I'll go to the studio and start laying down tracks for a couple of days." A workout magazine was lying on the table. "This reminds me. We are starting tomorrow morning on Deanne's gym. I believe we'll have some help, so it shouldn't take all day."

The front door blew open with an explosion of an eight-year-old running in. "Mom!" she yelled. The sudden interruption startled Madi.

"What is it? Slow down." Ally saw Michael sitting at the other end of the table.

"You have giant surfboards behind your house!" she said excitedly.

Madi glanced over at him. "You've been up for a while."

"Yep, we are going paddleboarding," he said, looking down at Ally. It was a miracle she wasn't terrified at the thought of getting back out into the water.

"Lenny, they have another one if you'd like to go?" he asked.

"No, it's okay—" she started.

"Come go with us," he interrupted.

A smile formed. "Okay."

"You go get ready and meet the three of us behind my cottage. We'll go get the other board," he said to Madi. Without arguing Madi vanished into her bedroom to get ready while the trio raced to the golf cart.

Before Madi could walk around Michael's cottage she could hear the excitement of the two girls. Rounding the corner she found the three of them playing "king of the surfboard" with Lenny tugging on his arm and Ally glued to his back. "Hey! You ready?" he asked Madi.

"I don't do boards, but I'll try," she said.

"The young kid said a monkey could do this. You're not going to let a monkey show you up?" He laughed.

With a quick raise of her eyebrows she said, "We'll see."

Dragging his and Ally's boards to the water he heard a voice coming from up the beach. "Dude, you the man!" Webster said walking up.

"You want to try it?" Michael asked, pointing at the boards.

"Noooo, you got three lady folks to take out. When the waves return you and I will go out," he said. Michael wasn't sure if he wanted the invitation to surf with Webster, since the old hippie would more than likely show him up.

They all waded out knee-deep in the emerald water and Lenny and Ally jumped on as though they had done this all their lives. It threw Michael off his coolness game in front of Madi. "Michael, I don't know," Madi started.

"It's nothing, watch this!" Seeing the girls climb on so quickly he expected the same results. What he didn't calculate was the weight difference between the little girls and a grown man. Holding his paddle he started on his knees and stood up with one foot forward and the other just touching the board before it shot out from underneath him like a cannonball. *Crap!* was the last thing he thought before landing flat on his back in the sparkling emerald water. As he reached both hands forward he felt the sudden pain on his back, and the instant redness forming from smacking the water.

He really didn't want to surface because he could hear the laughter from the three girls and possibly Webster. He broke the waterline slowly, looking at Madi who was doubled over. "Watch this?" She was laughing. Trying to save face he laughed too.

"Well, you try," he challenged her.

Madi gently climbed on her board and slowly stood up. "This isn't that hard." She was surprised.

"Hmm!" He sighed and slowly climbed back on.

After paddling around the shore and getting use to the boards, they paddled out toward another small island only a few football fields away. The sun was hot and Michael felt his skin turning red before they reach the island. Pausing for a small break Madi applied sunblock to the girls and then to Michael. He had stashed bottles of water in each life vest that was attached to the front of the boards. They played on the boards till lunch, and returned to Michael's cottage for a quick sandwich. For the rest of the day they played on the beach and paddled up and down the shore. "I have these till tomorrow if you would like to see the sunset from the water?" he asked Madi. She nodded her head with a smile.

Madi had arranged for Lenny to watch Ally while they enjoyed the evening. "Lenny, do you want to take my golf cart to the pizza place for you guys?" Michael asked.

Lenny's eyes lit up. "Yeah!" Michael had seen her drive her parents' golf cart around the island. With money in hand, a freshly charged golf cart, and the freedom of the island's ten square miles, the girls took off.

Michael grabbed both boards and walked them to the water. Madi followed, thankful that chivalry had not died with Michael. He held her paddle and waved toward her board with his hand. "My lady!" She took the paddle and wondered if they would have the same start as earlier today. Michael wondered the same thing.

Paddling out a ways they stopped and sat down on their boards. Their legs straddled the boards as they held hands, and once again he felt her anchor bracelet dangling over his wrist.

"We have seen many sunsets this summer," he said.

"Yep, and I wouldn't trade a one of them," she added. Smiling at him she leaned over to kiss him, the thought of pulling him in the water crossed her mind.

When she pulled his arm Madi went in with him, and upon surfacing he heard her laughing. "I'm sorry, I couldn't help it," she said.

"Yeah, right." He smirked. He climbed back on his board to find Madi also climbing on his board. "What are you doing?" he asked. Without answering him she straddled him, her legs dangling in the water beside his. Sitting in his lap and giving her more height she grabbed his head with both of her wet hands and embraced his lips with hers. They floated till dusk fell and slowly made their way back to the beach. Pulling their boards up on the sand, they lay down on her board and talked.

Michael noticed Madi sniffing, thinking the salt water had entered her nose. Breaking the kiss, she asked, "Do you smell that?" Michael got a strong whiff of the sweet odor, and looking over Madi's shoulder, he could see Webster and Sunshine sitting several yards away. As they sat up Webster greeted them with a thumbs-up. *Secluded island with no privacy!* he thought.

Chapter 47

Michael dropped the phone trying to answer the text from Robin. She and two other promoters had left the airport and were heading to the island for their initial setup. Looking in the mirror at his back, he was redder than he'd hoped. The previous day was fun, but too much sun didn't go well with his sleeping. He had arranged several people to meet at Deanne's and help move and clean up the debris, he wondered if Webster would be in any shape to help. As he stepped on the front porch he had trouble shutting his door while double-fisting two cups of coffee.

Webster sat in the passenger seat of his golf cart."Good morning, bro," he said.

"I thought you would be dragging today," Michael responded.

"Why so?"

"You were partying pretty early yesterday."

Webster gave him a funny look. "Man, I'm too old to party." Michael didn't question it; his definition of *partying* was probably wilder than he could imagine.

Madi locked the door behind her and made her way over to the cart. "Hi, Webster. You looked like you guys were having fun last night," she said.

"I've never stopped the honeymoon." He grinned. Michael

thought she had asked for that, but knew she hadn't been around Webster very much.

"Is Sunshine joining us?"

"She's going to show up at noon. Age is keeping her labor days down."

"Lenny and Ally went down with Lenny's parents. We can go on," Madi said. When they pulled up they were greeted by a larger group of people than they had expected. Some were already tearing apart lumber and stacking it along the street. It didn't call for much organization—just tear down and stack. Within an hour they had most of it already done, and some of the group started working on the adjacent building. Before they realized it their crew was working the entire street.

"Hey, Robin is on her way this morning," Michael said.

"What can I do to help?" Madi asked.

"I don't know yet. Well . . . " He stopped.

She turned toward him. "What?"

"Can you help me with supper tonight?" he asked.

"Of course," she said. She then pointed at Deanne and the young guy who waited tables at the pizza place. "He's been on her heels all morning."

That gave Michael an idea for lunch. He approached the young man. "Do you think your boss would have time if I ordered pizza for this group?"

The young guy smiled. "Yes, sir, and it's me."

"Me?"

"I own Island Pizza," he said politely.

Michael nodded his head. "Awesome. Twenty larges?"

"Yes, sir, coming right up. Deanne, I have to go cook," he said.

"I can help," she said in an innocent, flirtatious tone. Certainly not the tone Michael was used to when she trained him. The two vanished into the pizza place.

Randy, the owner of the bar and grill, stopped by and visited.

"We are back open," he let the crowd know. Michael picked up on the hint that he needed business.

"We'll be there tonight," Michael said.

Randy quickly asked, "Can you play?"

"Yeah, I'm sure I can come up with something."

Randy shook his hand and rushed off.

"That's your way of cooking?" Madi asked, grinning.

Michael's phone buzzed with a text. "Almost there. Where are you?" Robin texted.

"Island Pizza," he texted back.

"Yo, man, we got this place cleaned up super fast," Webster said wiping the sweat from his forehead.

A tan BMW pulled up and Robin and two others stepped out. She went straight for Michael, wrapping her arms around the sweaty New York City boy. "So, I see you planned a concert already. Why did you need me?" Robin said.

"I haven't done anything yet," he answered, confused.

"The marquee sign in front of Randy's Bar and Grill said you were playing tonight," one of the other men said.

Michael laughed inside, realizing that was why Randy was in such a hurry to leave. "Yeah, I guess I am."

They visited during the afternoon. Madi thought Robin was becoming colder toward her, but she wasn't sure why.

After cleaning up and resting for a short time, Michael walked over to Madi's while reading a text from Robin. "We are staying at Land Inn. I'm in room 204. We'll meet you at Randy's."

The sky had turned to a bright orange and a light breeze had picked up. Madi was reclining in a rocking chair on the front porch. Catching her smiling at him as he approached, he sank into her green eyes that peered out from her bangs.

When they pulled up to Randy's, the place was packed. Michael's first thought was if he'd known it was going to be this busy, he'd have cooked at home. Then he realized they were there to hear him play. Randy had reserved a table for them, which felt funny to Michael. A small clap was heard when he walked in, and many of the faces that greeted him were the islanders themselves.

After ordering appetizers he kissed Madi on the cheek. "I'm going to go play until our food gets here."

He pulled the bench up to the piano and played through a warm-up. Then thumping the microphone to see if it was on, he welcomed everyone. "Thanks for coming out. From the words of a visitor, you guys really do make this home and are one big family." He looked at Deanne. "So I would like to dedicate this first song to our fitness guru, Deanne." She blushed and lowered her head. Michael noticed she was holding hands with the young pizza entrepreneur. He played "Young Love"—a song of his that had won several awards.

The rest of the night he played without saying another word; he wanted his music to do all the talking. Madi sat at the table with her head perched in her hand, propped up on the table. Michael glanced her direction several times, and during one song he never took his eyes off her. She didn't know it was a new song he'd planned to reveal at the upcoming concert.

Taking a break to eat, Robin asked, "That last song was new."

"Yes, one of a few that I have written since staying here. And yes, you and Doug were right," he said before she had a chance to say anything.

After they ate he went back to the old piano. "I have a couple more songs, but before I start I want to let everyone know that we are having a benefit concert here on the island in three weeks with many other guests playing. So please tell all your friends," he said.

Finishing the last few songs he was ready to call it a night. *I just hope I can have some time with you*, he thought, looking at Madi.

Chapter 48

The next three weeks flew by with the excitement of the coming concert. With most of Michael's writing done, he was able to spend time with Madi. Deanne had reopened her gym with the help of the islanders, and her parents helped financially with a few extra things the insurance company didn't cover. Everything had turned back to its normal, slow-pace island life.

Lying on his couch reading an article on barrel racing in a magazine Madi had left at his cottage, Michael's phone buzzed with a text from Madi. "Come outside." He searched for his flip-flops and began walking to the door before they were firmly on his feet. When he opened the door he found Madi standing in her driveway beside two scooters with silver helmets hanging from the mirrors.

"What are you doing?" he shouted from his front porch.

"Asking you for a day date. Think you can ride one?" she asked, pointing at the scooter on her left.

"With my luck . . . no!" He laughed and made his way across the yard.

By the time he reached her drive, she was on a scooter and had it running. "Where are we going?" he asked.

"Just get on!"

"You know I have something tonight," he said, referring to

the benefit concert. She zipped off, leaving on a small cloud of white smoke in the drive. He quickly mounted the scooter, and after a moment of buckling his helmet he buzzed out after her. Initially driving slow for him to catch up, Madi looked over her shoulder and gave a smile that said, "Hurry up."

"You good?" she yelled at him.

"Yep!" he replied.

They sped through town, observing everyone setting up for the annual festival. It had conveniently been scheduled a month earlier to coincide with the benefit concert. The stagehands were erecting the stage at the foot of the island pier, and Michael thought of how they came close to losing Ally there just four weeks earlier. Madi wasn't bothered by the idea and had almost blocked the incident from her mind.

There was an old-fashioned carnival being set up down the street from the stage with a small Ferris wheel, booths, and other rides. Some of the workers were already out promoting with old costumes—red striped shirts and Gatsby-style hats. Madi was excited for tonight but had other things on her mind at the moment.

Michael followed as they crossed the temporary bridge and left the island. He pulled alongside her. "Where are you taking me?" he yelled over the small engines.

"You'll see!" she persisted. Turning down an old seashell road that hadn't looked traveled in years, they continued until they reached a shell-and-gravel road that turned back toward the ocean. Michael drove slowly, avoiding larger rocks in the road, and Madi stopped only for a second to look toward a small grove of pine trees. She aimed her scooter toward the trees and cautiously drove through them with Michael directly behind her.

As if they were in a dark cave emerging into the light, they came out onto a small secluded beach that led to the beautiful emerald water much like that outside Michael's cottage.

"How in the world did you find this place?" he asked, taking off his helmet.

"A little birdie told me," she replied in a childlike voice. She hung her helmet on the mirror of her scooter, and with one fluid motion pulled her tank top off and revealed the dark pink bikini top she had on.

"I hope you can swim in those," she said, nodding toward his shorts. She pulled down her short shorts and wore a matching bikini bottom. Without waiting on him she jogged to the water. He watched her small figure enter the water and wondered if she was teasing him. Without a shirt he made his way to the water and waded in knee-deep. He dove in headfirst.

When he surfaced in front of her, she giggled. He ran his fingers up the side of her body, and she flung her arms over his shoulder before he could fully stand. Batting her eyes and hoping he would catch the hint, she pulled herself up to his face. Locking lips, she began kissing him. They sank back down into the glistening water, kissing as he held her body against his.

Michael pulled away thinking he heard something, and when he looked to the shore he didn't see anything. Madi pulled his face back to hers and continued the kiss. The sound of tires driving over limbs and fallen leaves broke their kiss as they watched a truckload of teenagers driving up to their secluded beach. "First one in!" yelled a teenage boy in the back of the truck.

Madi looked back at Michael with a disappointed look.

"It's just not meant to be right now." He smiled.

ᘐᘓ

Robin looked at her phone. "It's almost five. Where is he? And why aren't you answering?" She was becoming frustrated with Michael. Her phone rang, and Doug's name appeared on the screen.

"How's the show?" he asked.

"Ugh! If Michael doesn't get here it won't happen!"

"Where is he?" Doug asked, knowing it wasn't like Michael to be late.

"He and Madi have disappeared somewhere."

"Relax, he'll show." He laughed.

"It's not funny! I swear this little girl is going to ruin his career," she said as a beep came through her speaker. "There he is now. I'll call you back." She switched lines, "Where are you!?"

"Sorry, we're on our way back," he shouted over the scooter.

Robin pulled the phone back and looked at it. "What's that noise?"

"Tell you later, be right there."

Robin wasn't sure she was looking at Michael as the two of them rode up on their scooters. "Robin, I'm sorry, it's my fault," Madi said. Robin wasn't sure where they had been, but looking at the girlish grin on Madi's face and the glow that encompassed her, she had a pretty good idea.

"You need to get in the trailer and get ready," Robin said, opening the trailer that had been brought in for the entertainers. Michael walked in.

"You too," Robin said waving, Madi to follow.

Madi's eyes opened wide at the people in the trailer sitting in front of mirrors. Others lounged on couches; many of them were her favorite bands and singers. She knew they were playing but never guessed she would be in their presence. Michael walked through, hugging and shaking hands with many of them. She followed like a lost kid in a mall, bumping into him a few times; he pulled her underneath his arm and in front of him as he introduced her.

"Ah, you're the rodeo girl," a guy said in a British accent.

"Yes," she squeaked out. It was a singer she had heard her whole life and even saw in concert once in Atlanta. Now he knew who she was! Madi was starstruck.

A voice from the front of the trailer called for a band. "You're up!" She heard the crowd erupt as they took the stage only feet from the trailer. Michael sat in a chair in front of the long mirror that stretched the length of the trailer.

"Ms. Coverton?" a young lady asked. Madi was a little shocked she knew her name.

"Yes?" Madi asked.

"Have a seat and I'll get you ready."

Madi looked confused. "For what?"

"Have a seat, sweetie," Michael insisted.

The lady began fixing her hair. "Ally is a beautiful little girl," the young lady said.

"Ally? You know my Ally?"

"I had the girls here earlier fixing their hair and makeup," she replied.

"It's okay, I set it up. Relax . . . breathe," Michael said.

Hearing the word *breathe* from him sent chills up her back. It was a word Cole had used often to calm her nerves.

Chapter 49

After they called for the second artist to come to the stage, Madi started wondering why she was in the chair getting her hair done. She first thought it was a nice gesture on Michael's part.

"Why am I here?" she asked Michael.

Without looking at her, he said, "We need to have our violinist looking pretty."

Madi's stomach sank and she almost peed herself. "What!?"

"You didn't bring your violin?" He paused for a short moment. "I'm just kidding. I thought it would be nice for you and Ally to have some pampering." Madi looked at the young lady.

"Can I borrow that?" She took a small towel and popped Michael on the calf. He laughed, rubbing his leg.

"You might have met your match," said a voice from behind them.

"Yes, I have," Michael replied, looking in the mirror at Madi.

The roar of the crowd grew louder as the trailer door opened.

"Mom!" Ally yelled across the trailer. Ally jumped beside her, looking at her from the mirror. Madi was speechless at the sight of her little eight-year-old with her hair and makeup done.

"You look beautiful!" Madi managed to say.

"Thanks, but do you know who's playing right now!?" she exclaimed.

"I do." Madi smiled back.

"Hurry up and come join me and Lenny. We have special seats." Ally didn't give her any chance before she disappeared out the door and back to the stage.

Michael heard the soft words from Madi. "Thank you."

"You're welcome. I'm glad I was able to share this moment with you. I'm glad we have been able to share this summer together," he added.

"Oh, Ms. Coverton, please don't cry," the young lady said, dabbing Madi's tears with a tissue.

"Sorry, they're happy tears," Madi said.

A voice from the front of the trailer yelled, "Mr. Curry, five minutes."

Madi looked at him. "You're going on now?"

"Yes." He smiled. "You didn't think they were opening for me, did you?" Michael ducked into a small changing room and reappeared with his signature black slacks and black button-down shirt with his sleeves rolled up.

"You ready?" He held his hand out for Madi; her eyes came alive like a little girl being kissed for the first time.

"Yeah."

Stepping down from the trailer steps Madi got her first real glimpse of the crowd in front of the stage—a sea of people stretched throughout the streets and more than a block deep. The rooftops of the local business had people stand and sitting on the edge with a front row seats to the concert.

Robin walked up and hugged Michael. "Have a good show," she said.

"These free shows are getting to be a pain in my side!" Robin said under her breath. Madi thought she heard Robin but blew it off as her imagination. Still, Robin shot a glare at her as the two passed by.

The artist before was walking down the stairs. "Michael,

you are the man. Lots of fun. Thank you for inviting me," he said as sweat rolled off his entire body.

Madi grabbed Michael's hand and drew it close to her chest. He turned to her and leaned down to kiss her, only to find her stopping him.

"I want to say something first." He straightened back up and gave her his attention. "There are many things that I have come to lose over the last few years—Cole, my faith, trust, and almost my little girl. I don't know if God has a plan for me—maybe it's fate, I don't know. My future was a blur, maybe even nonexistent until we came here to this tiny island. You've brought back something that I had thought I lost. You gave me the one thing I feared I would never get back. Hope! From the bottom of my heart, thank you."

Michael didn't move and stared into her eyes, giving her his undivided attention.

"Michael." She took his other hand and held them both close to her heart. "I love you!"

Everything around him went silent. Everyone around him disappeared. When he blinked again, Michael found himself standing in one of the fields similar to Madi's hay fields, confused and disoriented. He spun around, and as far as he could see there were fields of lush green grass that changed to a purple tint with the wind blowing through them. One minute he was standing with Madi about to go on stage, and the next he was in a weird dream. Off in the distance he saw a figure walking toward him—a male figure he didn't recognize. As he got closer Michael could see that he was tall, well-built, young, and good-looking, with a peaceful disposition.

Michael asked, "Who are you, and where are we?"

"You are in a place of imaginational magic," the figure said.

"You're Cole!" Michael knew as soon as he heard the words.

"I am."

"I don't think I understand," Michael said.

"You will," Cole replied.

"Have a seat," Cole said, sitting down in the thick knee-high grass. Michael sat down, still confused by what he was experiencing. "Michael, I always prayed that if something happened to me that my girls would be taken care of, and . . . well, something happened." Cole paused, looking down at the grass. "Madi is a special girl who is more faithful than anyone you will ever meet. She deserves a man who will love her unconditionally. Ally is in the most impressionable years of her life, and she needs a father who will love her and raise her to be like her mother. You are that man."

Michael tried to swallow but found the lump in his throat too big. "And you're okay with this?" he asked Cole.

Cole smiled and replied in a soft voice, "Yes."

"I never intended to come to Wilkes Key and find someone," Michael replied.

"People don't find love; it finds them."

"I don't know if I'm ready for this. What if she's not ready?" Michael said.

"We are all ready. And once that commitment is made, then we'll all experience peace," he answered Michael. Cole stood up. "I know you'll know what to do. Take care of my little girl." He started to walk off.

"Will I see you again?" Michael asked.

"Not after that commitment is made."

Michael turned toward the warm breeze, then turned back to find Cole gone.

Within a blink of an eye he found himself back at the concert standing in front of Madi. He hesitated for a brief moment to get his bearings back. Once he realized where he was, he said, "I love you too, Madi!" He embraced her and held her tight.

To her something felt different. It wasn't the same hug or the way he had held her before. *This is so strange . . . he's holding me like . . . like Cole did.* She laid her head on his chest and felt his heart racing. "I love you!" she repeated in a whisper.

"Michael! You're on!" said a man dressed in black with a headset.

"Good luck," she softly said.

"Thank you." He kissed her and took the stage. The crowd exploded with his wave to the sea of people.

"Thank you for coming out and helping support my friends of Wilkes Key. This night is for the people I've met on this island." He looked at Madi, "All of them."

A small band joined him onstage and he went right into his first song. The night became electrified, and Madi thought there would be no way for anyone to follow him. She sat beside Ally, who had been holding her chair. Michael's performance was eccentric and magical, and Madi and Ally swayed with every key struck on the baby grand.

At his conclusion he stood and thanked the crowd. Madi stood, applauding with everyone, and received a kiss blown from the man she had confessed her love to earlier.

Stepping offstage Ally ran and jumped into his arms. "What did you think?" he asked her.

"That was awesome," she said as her feet dangled off the ground.

Madi knew this was right.

As the British band lit the night with familiar sounds and fast entertainment, Michael and Madi stood close to the stage arm in arm. Madi leaned over to Lenny. "Can you make sure Ally gets to bed? Michael and I will be at the beach."

"Yes, ma'am," she replied.

Looking back at Michael, she yelled in his ear. "Come on. I have something else I want to show you." Making it back to the scooters they had brought, they followed the back roads to his cottage. They parked the scooters near the garage, and Madi barely gave him time to hang his helmet. "I overheard the stagehands talking about tonight's show and the finale." She pulled him to the beach.

They sat down near the water in the dry, powdery sand.

Facing town, she tucked her arms under his and leaned into him. They could see the stage lights beaming into the night sky, and they still heard music as if they were standing beside the stage. During the last song a single flare shot into the air, trailed by gold sparkles. Reaching its height it exploded into the first of many colored fireworks.

"Wow!" Michael replied. "I didn't even know they were shooting fireworks. You are surprising me today." She scooted to her knees and crawled in his lap to face him. They began kissing and fell back to the sand. Michael looked up only momentarily, scanning the beach for their hippie friends until Madi pushed him back down into the sand to continue their kiss. Through her hair draped over his face, he could see the fireworks exploding into bright colors over Wilkes Key.

Chapter 50

Taking a deep breath and stretching her arms over her head, Madi woke with an uncontrollable smile. She had finally gained the courage to tell Michael she loved him. She played the scene in her head over and over again, only to cause herself to giggle. *Oh my gosh!* Last night had been something from a fairy tale, from the secluded beach, to the concert, to the fireworks, to their night on the beach. She climbed out of bed and put her pajama bottoms on and slipped into a robe, leaving it untied. She quietly left the room, so as not to disturb Ally from sleeping. She felt as though she was floating to the kitchen, and pouring her coffee, she found herself giggling again.

She curled up on the couch and held her coffee close to her face, feeling the warmth surround her cheeks. She quietly talked to Gus who had crawled from his cage to the couch. With every chirp and beep his body would shake. She took another deep breath and exhaled with the joy of peace, not being able to sit still anymore she poured another cup, tied her robe, and headed across the street to Michael's. She thought it would be sweet to wake him if he was still asleep, and she knew his coffeemaker would be going. As she stepped onto the blacktop she couldn't stop smiling. Last night had been one of her most incredible nights to ever share.

She didn't recognize the white four-door Lexus parked in

the drive, but since the concert people had been in and out, she said a little prayer that he'd be alone. Just in case, she decided to lightly knock first. To her surprise the door opened.

Standing in the doorway was a tall, dark-haired, very attractive woman holding a coffee mug and wearing the long-sleeved black shirt that Michael had worn to the concert. Madi didn't know what to say. Her first thought was that there might be another couple visiting she didn't know about.

"Um, hi. Is Michael up?" Madi questioned.

The young woman smiled with a devious expression. "Yes, but he's in the shower. Can I help you?"

Madi was still confused, but she heard the noise of the shower. "Well, I was just checking on him." She paused, then said, "I'm Madi," hoping that would provide some clarity. But it only brought forth a shockwave.

"Hi, Madi, I'm Tessa. Michael's fiancée. Are you a friend of Michael's?"

Madi went numb. First she thought maybe she misheard her. Tessa leaned on the door frame, obviously blocking Madi's way. When she did she revealed the red panties she had on under Michael's black shirt.

Madi blinked. "I live across the street," she mumbled.

"Okay, well he's tired from the concert and all. So I'll let him know that you stopped by." Tessa shut the door in Madi's face.

Tessa walked back to the living area and lay across the couch. She crossed her legs and positioned his black shirt to reveal her panties. Leaning her head back and shaking her hair straight she unbuttoned the top two buttons, revealing her cleavage. The bathroom door opened and Michael walked out, wrapped in a towel and drying his hair with another hand towel.

"Whoa!" he screamed as he jumped back. "Tessa! What the hell are you doing here?" he blurted.

"Well, it's nice to see you too. I was hoping for a better

response, but I know we have some work to do on our relationship."

"Relationship? We ended that over a year ago. How did you find me?" he asked.

She stood up and seductively approached him. "You're a star. It's not hard finding you. Now, let's start this off right." She grabbed the front of his towel. He removed her hand and glanced out front, knowing her presence could cause all sorts of trouble.

She noticed him staring to the front. "Oh, yeah. Your neighbor just stopped by. I told her that you would be busy. You don't need fans hanging around today."

"Who? Madi!?" he yelled. She rolled her eyes. "Get your clothes on and get the hell out of here! Or should I have the police escort you out?"

He quickly ran to his room and slipped into a pair of shorts, pulling a shirt over his head. He wasn't thinking about Tessa leaving; he just wanted to get to Madi. He ran across the street barefoot and knocked on the front door, again and again. "Madi! Let me explain. Madi!" No answer. He looked in the front windows and then walked to the side. Her Jeep was still parked in the drive. Knocking one last time, he yelled, "Madi! Please listen to me." He was unaware that Madi was just inside, sitting against the door, balled up and sobbing uncontrollably.

Walking back across the street Tessa met him on the front porch in her clothes. "I don't know what happened between us, but I am willing to give it another try. Here's where I'm staying. Call." She handed him a card.

He walked in and slammed the door behind him. Not looking at the card he wadded it up and threw it across the counter.

He picked up his phone and tried to call Madi, but it went straight to voice mail. He tried texting, "Please call!" Pacing the room and running his hand over his head, he tried to get his wits under control.

Madi stood in front of her bathroom mirror, franticly shaking, not able to process what just happened. *Michael said she was not part of his life, that he hadn't seen her in a year. Maybe I'm wrong . . . but she was in his shirt and her panties . . . and he was in the shower! I am the biggest fool!*

Ally, sleepy-eyed and confused, stood in the hallway watching her mother's heart unravel.

"Did the key work?" Robin asked Tessa as she walked by her hotel room.

"Yes, it did. He was in the shower when I got there," Tessa replied.

"Well?" Robin asked.

"Let's just say it couldn't have worked out any better. The little hussy came knocking . . . and well, I gave her a good show."

Robin grinned. "That's worth my money," she said under her breath.

Tessa opened her door with her key card and looked toward Robin. "And don't worry—Michael still doesn't know," Tessa said.

"Here." Robin handed her a thick envelope with cash.

"Thank you. Call anytime." Tessa grinned and disappeared into her room.

Robin went to her room and grabbed her phone. "Great concert last night. What are your plans today?" she texted Michael.

"A disastrous morning. Tessa is here! I've got to patch things with Madi," he sent back.

"Come here first! I can help," she replied.

Michael was still confused. "Okay. Give me thirty minutes."

Robin set the phone down and smiled. "Now for a little phone call to Ms. Georgia to make sure she leaves!"

Chapter 51

Madi's jeep turned onto the interstate. She tried her best to hide everything from Ally, but she knew Ally was smarter than that.

"I'm going to miss Gus," Ally said.

"Yeah, me too. But we'll visit him," Madi replied.

She had left Lenny in charge of watching after Gus until her father's friends returned back home to the cottage in less than two weeks. She couldn't get the words out of her head that Robin had planted during a nasty phone call: "Tessa was never out of the picture." She heard them over and over.

Her phone rang. Looking down she saw it was James. "Hi, Dad."

"How far are you?" he asked.

"We just got on the interstate, so four and a half hours."

"Okay, drive safe. Your mother and I love you," he said.

Madi turned up the volume on the radio. She knew the pain of a broken heart and of losing someone, but this pain was different. *I trusted him!*

Michael sat on the beach staring out at the ocean. The waves had picked up and the crashing sound had returned. Lady waddled up beside him and sat close. She sensed something was wrong. "Well, Lady, we started this summer together and it looks like we'll end it together." She lay down, placing her head in his lap.

"I always said that man's best friend was a dog," Webster said, walking up. "You mind?" He pointed to the sand next to Michael.

"No, have a seat."

"Man, tough few days," Webster replied.

"Yep," Michael said.

"Bro, I've learned a lot of things over my days. But the most insightful advice is to treat women like doves."

Michael looked at him for more of an explanation but it never came. They sat silently and stared into the endless sea for what seemed like hours.

Webster stood back up. "Gonna miss you, bro. Stay in touch."

Webster placed his hand on Michael's shoulder.

"Thanks, Webster. Tell Sunshine bye for me."

He watched as the old hippie kicked sand as he walked back to his blue cottage on stilts. His long gray hair, thick leather skin, and casual walk told his story.

"Well, sweet Lady, you want to walk through with me one last time?" He stood to his feet and brushed the sand off his shorts. Opening the screen door he made his way around the baby grand piano that was covered with blue moving blankets. The cottage was spotless and quiet, and the sun beamed a ray of light through the kitchen window. Michael could see small particles floating in the air.

He left a note on the counter and set his key on the paper, then walked out the front door, locking it behind him. Lady followed him down the stairs and to his car. Bending down on one knee, he said, "I wish I could take you with me. Thanks for a great summer." He rubbed both sides of her face. With her eyes wide and sagging she let out a faint, whimpering cry.

As he pulled out, he looked in his rearview mirror to see

that she was still sitting in the same spot watching him drive off. He passed in front of Deanne's and honked as he drove by, and he saw her training someone through the new windows that had been installed.

Jenny was parked near Randy's. "You heading out?" she asked as he rolled down his window.

"Yep, it's time."

"Sorry you're leaving alone." Jenny smirked.

"Me too. You've got my number. Call if you guys ever need anything." She waved as he pulled off.

As he drove over the temporary bridge, tears formed in his eyes. His stomach felt empty and his heart pounded. *This didn't end the way I had expected.*

His music muted as his phone rang over the speakers. It was Robin. "Hey, Robin."

"How are you doing?"

"Heading out now."

"I'm sorry things didn't work out."

"Me too," he replied.

"Well, I don't think Madi was ready. She wouldn't be acting this way if she was. I'm sorry," she said.

"Yeah, I think you're right." He looked back as he drove around a corner and watched the welcome sign to Wilkes Key Island disappear. "I'll be home in a few days," he said.

"Drive safe. We have a lot of things to do when you get here," Robin replied over the phone. He pushed a button to hang up, and his music returned.

Reaching for his glasses in the passenger seat he knocked over the bag of things he had collected off the countertop. A wadded-up piece of paper fell out. Not sure what it was he unfolded it to see it was the card Tessa had given him. He pulled over. "Land Inn, room 201. Wasn't that the place Robin stayed? Room 204?" he said aloud.

Then it hit him. Everything Robin had said about Madi and to Madi, the evil looks—it was all adding up.

He just stared at the crumpled-up card and tried to wrap his head around the thought of Robin sabotaging his relationship. *Why?* Then the past began unfolding in his mind—the coldness toward Doug, how controlling she was of his shows, the show profits, and the delay in sending money to the orphanage. *Is she really this cold? Is she only worried about money? Did she take me in for her benefit?!* Michael was never an angry person, but the blood in his veins began to boil. *She used me!* The very thought made him sick to his stomach. Thinking about his next move he picked up the phone and dialed Doug's number.

Doug picked up after the third ring. "Rough few days," he said before Michael could say anything.

"Yeah. Are you alone?" Michael asked.

After a pause, he said, "Yes. What's the matter?"

"Tell me that I'm imagining that Robin sent Tessa to my cottage."

After a longer pause on the phone, Doug said, "Michael, I wouldn't put it past her."

"Why!?" Michael could hear Doug take a deep breath; Doug had dreaded the day he had to explain Robin's motives to him.

"She is a user. She'll use anyone for money. I know she thought Madi would have an impact on you settling down and possibly retiring."

"Why would she care? She should know I'll always take care of her financially."

"She doesn't see it that way. You stop doing shows and there goes her 20 percent."

Michael thought for a moment. "She's handled a lot of my money, money that was to go to the orphanage and other causes."

"It always got there," Doug replied.

"What about you?" Michael asked with a more aggressive tone.

"What about me?"

"Why didn't you tell me?"

"Well . . . I guess I was scared of losing her. She had planned to leave me when I had my accident, up until she learned the general was writing me into his will." The words from Doug brought Michael's blood pressure up.

"Why didn't you leave her!?" he nearly shrieked into the phone.

"I guess it's because I needed someone."

They were silent for a moment.

"So her motives for moving me in with you guys when I was sixteen?"

Doug interrupted him. "All for her!"

Wow! If I wasn't so mad this would hurt.

"She's going to have to call Madi and explain all this," Michael demanded.

"She'll never do it," Doug assured him.

Michael shook his head in disbelief. "And you're staying with her?" he asked Doug.

"I don't have a choice. Who is going to take care of this old cripple?"

"I would," Michael replied.

"No, you have a life to live. Don't worry about me—I'm taken care of."

"Doug, you know that this will end our relationship."

"Stay in touch with me, Michael. I've always cared about you. I'm sorry I let you down over this," Doug replied.

Michael hung up the phone and pulled back out onto the road. A new determination rushed through his veins.

ᘓᘐ

Over the next few days Michael had time to plan his future tour and his predicament with Robin. She had given him so much and helped him become a star, but she had robbed him of the one thing he had searched for his whole life. What was greater—his success or the girl he'd fallen in love with? By the time he got home, he had made arrangements to start his new tour with a new manager and was within hours of firing the one he had.

ᴓ

With a dust cloud fading, Madi stepped off Bay. “He looks good, kiddo!” James replied from the side of the arena.

She led Bay out the gates. “Yep, he feels good. Another week and we’ll be ready to hit some shows.”

James climbed down and walked over to Madi. “She’s not going to be far behind you.” He pointed at Ally, who rode Grey into the arena for her practice run.

“Nope, she’s got the heart of her daddy and your bravery.” Madi wiped the sweat off her forehead.

“Bravery can be covered up,” James replied.

“Oh, please, you’ve never been scared of anything your whole life.”

“A man without fears isn’t a man,” he said. She smiled as she took the reins off Bay. “And pain can’t be covered up either,” he added. She ignored the comment but knew he was right.

“So you girls going to hit the rodeo next week?” he asked.

“That’s the plan.”

“Don’t you think you should get Bay in better shape?”

“It’s time to go,” she snapped. James didn’t say anything else; he knew she’d already made up her mind.

“What did you think?” Ally yelled from the arena about her practice run.

“You’re going to win ’em all!” He shouted back.

He walked up to the house and onto the front porch where Rena met him. “She’s really hurting,” she said.

He turned and watched her disappear into the barn with Bay. “Yep, she is.”

Chapter 52

"A night with Michael Curry?" Muturi said as he stepped on Michael's tour bus.

"Sounds like prostitution, doesn't it? How's my friend?" Michael said, hugging him.

"Good. Ready for this tour. And in the south of the states?"

"You're going to love it. Plus the weather isn't any different than Tanzania's."

"Hot and dry?" Muturi asked.

"Hot." Michael said. He loved Muturi's accent and appreciated his lack of knowledge with the US.

"So, I hear good things about this new album," Muturi said, picking up a CD. "*Fields of Alicia*. Tell me about it."

The bus hissed as the driver put it into drive and pulled out for the four-month tour. "It's good old classical stuff with a little bit of fight," Michael said.

"I know your music. I mean, the titles and the songs. No artist just comes up with a name."

Michael took a deep breath, trying his hardest to hide the pain. It had been a long few weeks with studio time, changing managers, and the fallout from Robin's actions. Many nights he would wake up and walk out onto his balcony wondering how Madi was, and not an hour went by he didn't think about them both.

"Michael?" Muturi waved his hand in front of him holding Michael's CD.

"Sorry. *Fields of Alicia*, huh?"

"Yeah."

"Did you know that there is a certain grass named Alicia Bermuda and it was brought over from Africa?"

"I did not know that," Muturi replied. Michael sank down into the leather couch and propped his feet up.

"The first song, 'Lady's Friend,' was written for a special friend I made on the island this summer. You could say that I fell in love with her. She was always there and had a unique sense of wisdom." His mind faded off to the island. He remembered meeting Lady for the first time; she must have known that Gus was secretly a devil bird because she had always kept her distance.

"I lived down the street from the most eccentric hippie you will ever meet. Life to him was just one giant wave that he was riding. He said sometimes it's fast and other times it's smooth. Loyal and a true romantic to his wife." He imagined Webster and Sunshine dancing on their wooden deck, even in old age. They truly knew what love was and created peace around it. Michael's eyes began to tear up. "That's how I came up with 'Hippie Sunrise,'" he whispered.

"'Sharks!' It's an upbeat song. It came to me while fishing for sharks and the funny story that came out of it." He thought back to when the bucket of blood hit the floor. He would never forget the captain's expression. *Priceless!*

"I witnessed a hurricane. My first and hopefully my last. But sitting on the beach and watching it come was beautiful." He imagined the touch of Madi's hand against his. The howling wind and sideways rain, seeing her run after him across the street as they checked on his cottage. She was laughing and soaking wet. *She would have gone anywhere with me.* "That's 'Violently Beautiful,' named after the storm," Michael said, wiping his eyes.

Muturi listened intensely to Michael's stories and watched the tears run down his face. "The fourth song is 'Cowboy's Piano.' I've got to take you to a country bar with two-stepping and steel guitars. I thought I could prove that I was as tough as they were. But not being from their ground, well . . . don't play another man's game." Michael could almost see Madi peeking through the dance floor at him as he played Pat's keyboard and sang county music. He remembered her staring up at him while they danced and her straight hair falling back as she swayed back and forth. The memory brought a lump to his throat.

Michael never noticed the tears that were soaking the collar of his shirt; he was entranced by his memories as he told the story. "The fifth song is 'Endless Sea of Green.' I hope we have time to see a hay field."

"A hay field?" Muturi asked.

"It's part of farming, you know. Hay. But the one farm I visited seemed to have powers over your mind. The fields looked just like an ocean, and the wind would blow the grass to make it look like waves." Michael thought back to Madi lying beside him in the fields and how she kissed him. *So innocent and so real. Her lips were perfect.*

Michael was quiet for a while, but Muturi urged him on. "What about this 'Angels in the Fields'?"

Michael blinked a few times to clear his vision. "Very powerful." He leaned over and looked at Muturi. "Have you ever seen an angel?"

Muturi thought for a moment. "No, I don't think so."

He rolled back over to his back. "I have. Strong, full of truth, and mysterious." He drifted back to when Madi told him that she loved him and he found himself in the fields. That would be a story and conversation to take to the grave since he had a great appreciation for Cole. *I'm sorry for failing you.*

"The seventh song is 'Imaginational Magic'! I almost named the album after this song," Michael said.

"I like it."

"So dynamic and mighty, it was truly magical. These fields would take you anywhere in the world you wanted to go—in your imagination." The swaying of the tour bus felt like the swinging of Madi's wicker porch swing, where she had told him all about her childhood and the fields being her safe place. Listening to her, he could almost she her in pigtails and glasses at the same age as Ally. *Tomboy, huh?*

"Which brings me to the name of the album, *Fields of Alicia*." He paused. "It's a beautiful piece that starts with a violin, and then the piano takes over only to be passed by the violin again. The two instruments go back and forth in a playful manner, and the song ends with the two entwined." Now he faded off, seeing only Madi's face. He visualized her on the secluded beach, the day that they had rented paddleboards, carrying debris from Deanne's—the visions kept coming.

"So when are you going after her?" Muturi's words pulled Michael out of his trance.

"What?" he asked.

"When are you going after this Madi?" Michael didn't remember telling Muturi her name.

"I don't think I can," Michael said.

"That's not what you believe! It ends with the two entwined." Muturi smiled.

Chapter 53

"Come on, Mom!" Ally shouted from the bleachers in Austin, Texas. Madi was holding Bay back at the entrance to the arena, and she could hear her number-one cheerleader screaming her name.

"Okay, Bay, let's prove to this world what we've got." Bay jerked his head forward, begging for her to release him; his feet pranced in one spot. She gave him the reins. Dirt flew out from under his hooves as he dug in for an explosion of a start. Into his second stride he stretched out his long neck, his mane and tail blowing behind him. When he entered the arena he gained speed at the flashing cameras.

Setting in and pushing off, he felt the first barrel breeze his hip. Grabbing all the dirt he could with his front hooves he bolted to the second barrel. He engulfed it!

He could hear the cheering coming from Ally: "Go, Bay!"

He pressed on faster than he'd ever felt. Feeling the tap on the corner of his mouth he knew Madi was asking for everything. Two strides and he felt the third standing as he gained speed.

"Come on, boy, run . . . run!"

Bay's eyes watered as he gained speed toward the finish beam in the arena. Within feet from the timer and with Bay fully stretched out, Madi looked up at the timer.

"Almost there . . ."

Crossing she heard the rodeo announcer scream, "A new arena record!"

"Yes, yes, yes! We did it!" she screamed coming down the alleyway. Bay felt the tug on both sides of his mouth—the run was over. He sensed that he had done something good. He eased up, and upon exiting the alley, he took one step that didn't feel right. In a split-second, Bay's front legs buckled under him.

"Mommy!" Madi heard Ally from behind just before she met the ground. She had no time to brace herself. The pain was sudden and intense and she thought she heard the announcer asking for the paramedics. Then everything went black.

She felt someone tugging on her arm. "Ally?" she squeaked out.

"Lie still, I'm putting in an IV," she heard.

Her eyes still blurry, she said, "Ally? Where's Ally?"

"I have her," a familiar voice said. Madi recognized her fellow competitor holding Ally. She then realized she was on a stretcher in the back of an ambulance.

"Bay! How's Bay?" she asked.

"Please lie still, you've suffered head trauma," the paramedic said.

"How's Bay?" she screamed.

"Mom!" Ally was crying. Madi watched another EMT start to close the doors. She then saw a few people standing near Bay who was still on the ground. *Why is he still down? He should be up!*

"Bay!" she screamed as the doors shut.

She felt the needle in her arm. "Please hold still so I can start the IV and get you some meds." The back of the ambulance started spinning, and then a strong pain grew in her chest as she gasped for air.

"Let's go! Let's go!" the paramedic urgently shouted.

ꙮ

A few days later a convoy of semis and tour buses entered into the city of Austin, Texas. Michael had kicked back on the leather couch where he'd grown accustomed to watching their satellite TV. He was staring outside the windows at the buildings coming into sight when he heard the sports broadcaster's voice. "More on the story of the comeback professional cowgirl that took a tragic twist. Madi Coverton had just set the new arena record here in Austin, Texas, this past Saturday night when her horse fell, causing both of them to crash just outside the arena. If you know the name it's because Madi Coverton was well on her way to winning the finals a few years ago when her husband was killed in a farming accident. Now, three years later, it seems that tragedy has struck again. For more on the story, here's Nancy Seater."

Michael felt sick as he jumped up in a panic. "Get me to Georgia!" he demanded.

Chapter 54

A light wind blew through the grass, but this time there was a chill to the air. "Looks like old man winter is coming early this year," James said to Ally, who was sitting on a few bales of hay on the trailer. She was working on tying two pieces of grass together. She was quiet and somber.

"It's not like you to be quiet. Has the cat got your tongue?" he said, trying to break a grin on her face.

She didn't say anything. It was a familiar look that he remembered seeing when she had lost her daddy. *God, this little girl doesn't deserve this type of learning*, James prayed.

"Grandpa?" she asked.

"Yes, darling?"

"Why does love hurt so much?" she asked.

"Well, I guess that's just part of love. But, you know, it's much stronger on the other end."

"What?" she asked.

"You see, love is powerful and has many emotions, but the happiness it brings outweighs the pain." He hoped he wasn't confusing her but thought she was too young to know that. *Little girls should only have to worry about butterflies and bugs.*

"Why don't you come down from there and go tell Gran that I'll be in for supper soon?" he said. She didn't argue and jumped down from the hay trailer handing him the grass she had braided together. "Thank you. You know your mom used to do the very same thing?" he said.

"I know," she said as she walked toward the house with her head down.

James took a deep breath and faced the fields; they were losing their color. "A lot of hurt has come over this farm in the last few years. Don't you think it's time to give it a rest?" he said toward the sky. He walked out to the one field that hadn't yet been cut.

Ally reached the front porch. "Grandpa said he'd be in shortly."

"Okay, dear, go wash up." Rena looked out at the fields and watched her husband. With the sunset soon approaching she wondered how long his strength would stay with the family losing so much. She knew he took everything to heart.

"Hey, kiddo, I miss having you around," he said, running his hand over the tall grass. He figured he would be able to get another cut before the cold set in, but hated to cut the last field for Madi's sake.

"I'm still here, Dad. It's gonna take more than a concussion to take me out," Madi said, lying in the field.

"You've gone through more grief than anyone should have to go through. And if I could take it away I would."

"I know, Dad. Thank you."

"Is there someone you want to talk to?"

"A therapist?" she asked.

"Well, something like that."

"No, I'll be fine."

"You know what fine means to me?" he said. He'd always said that *fine* stood for frantic, insane, nuts, and egotistical.

"I know. But I'm okay," she assured him.

He stood over her thinking and praying. "Please let me know what I can do."

"I will," she answered. "I miss him." Tears ran down her face.

"I know," James replied.

"Come to the house when you're ready," James said looking up; then he abruptly turned and walked away.

He sure left quickly, she thought, knowing that her dad liked to hang around the fields. She took another deep breath and closed her eyes, hoping that a warm breeze would pass by. She had given up on praying for it.

James ducked under the barbed-wire as he exited the field and smiled at the man who walked past him.

Madi was still on her back, concentrating on her breathing and waiting for the wind. *Just one more warm breeze, please.*

She heard footsteps and thought her father had returned when she heard an unexpected voice coming from the field. "A friend once told me treating a woman like a dove would solve many problems. I didn't understand at first until I read a little on them; it turns out that doves mate for life. They build their nest together, they raise babies together, and the male dove will even fight for the female. I know it sounds stupid, but I'm fighting for you," Michael said, kneeling on both knees beside her with tears in his eyes.

At first she thought he was a vision, then she realized he was real. Tears poured from her eyes too. "Did Webster tell you that?"

"Yes."

Madi broke into a violent sob and laid there a moment, her hands covering her face in disbelief.

Michael pulled her body up and into his, whispering, "I've got you."

"Please keep me!" she cried.

"I will, Madi. I love you!" The words penetrated deep into her soul, and for the first time since the night on the beach, she felt her heart beat again.

"I want you and Ally. I want a family . . . your family." Tears fell freely from his eyes.

She pulled back. "What are you saying?"

"Marry me!"

She just stared through blurry vision, unable to talk. She tried to say what she wanted but it wouldn't come out. She finally nodded, lips quivering and tears steadily flowing. She wrapped her arms around him and buried her face into his neck; he lifted her into his arms and carried her out of the field. The warmth of his chest and his strong heartbeat flooded her with peace.

Once he reached the edge of the uncut field he turned back to face the sun setting over the hay. A warm breeze picked up and blew all around them.

"Michael!" a voice screamed from behind. Ally was running toward them.

"Set me down," Madi asked—just in time, as Ally leaped into Michael's arms.

"You're back!" she said.

"Yes I am. And I'm not going anywhere, I promise." He looked at her eyes and found them also filled with tears.

"I missed you," her little voice quivered.

"I missed you both so much," he whispered into her tangled hair.

Madi wrapped her arms around both of them and closed her eyes. *Thank you!*

ඏ

Walking back to the house as a family, Michael noticed Bay grazing in a nearby field with his right front leg wrapped in vet wrap.

He looked out across the blue-green waves of grass one last time as the orange sun blinked over the horizon, and caught a glimpse of Cole. They locked eyes for a moment, and Michael nodded in thanks and acceptance.

Cole nodded back, smiled, and faded into the field.